Emergency Exit

Books by Clarence Major

Emergency Exit
Reflex and Bone Structure
The Syncopated Cakewalk
The Dark and Feeling
NO
The Cotton Club
Symptoms and Madness
Private Line
Dictionary of Afro-American Slang
Swallow the Lake
The New Black Poetry
All-Night Visitors

Emergency Exit

Clarence Major

Fiction Collective  New York

Emergency Exit

First Edition

Library of Congress Catalog number: 79-52031
ISBN: 0-914590-59-6 (paperback)
ISBN: 0-914590-58-8 (hardback)

Published by: Fiction Collective, Inc.
Production by: Coda Press, Inc.
Distributed by: George Braziller, Inc.
                  One Park Avenue
                  New York, New York 10016

The publication of this book is in part made possible with support from the National Endowment for the Arts, the Committee on University Scholarly Publications of the University of Colorado at Boulder, the New York Council on the Arts; and with the cooperation of Teachers and Writers Collaborative, New York, and the Department of English, University of Washington at Seattle.

Reproductions of some paintings here originally appeared in *Black American Literature Forum*, Vol. 13, No. 2 (Summer, 1979) and in *par rapport* (Winter, 1979).

The photograph of the author is used with consent, courtesy of Sharyn Jeanne Skeeter.

ACKNOWLEDGMENTS

Portions of this book were previously published as follows:

"A Life Story," *Essence*, 2/10 (February, 1972)

"Drama in Flames," *Some*, 4 (Summer, 1973)

"Realism: A Dark Light," *Chelsea*, 32 (1973)

"Just Think Survival," *B.O.P.* (1974)

"Social Work," *The Black Scholar*, Vol. 6, No. 9 (June, 1975)

"All-American Cheese," *Seems*, Nos. 6 & 7 (Summer, 1975)

"Excerpts from Inlet," *Agni*, No. 7 (Summer, 1976)

"Excerpts from Inlet," *Bachy*, 8 (1976)

"First," and "Nonrepresentational," *Capstan* (1976)

"Emergency Exit," *Dark Waters*, Vol. 3, No. 1 (Fall, 1977)

"Emergency Exit," *Afterthought Magazine*, Vol. 1, No. 1, (1978)

"Excerpts from Emergency Exit," *The New Earth Review*, 5 & 6 (1978)

"Inlet," *Statements 2* (New York: George Braziller, 1978)

"Excerpts from Emergency Exit," *Obsidian*, Vol. IV, No. 2 (1978)

"Excerpts from Emergency Exit," *Hand Book*, No. 3 (1979)

"Bones," *Black American Literature Forum*, Vol. 12, No. 1, Summer 1978

Note: All references to actual people are fictional. All references to fictional characters are real.

DEDICATION

To the people whose stories do not hold together

"I mistrust all frank and simple people, especially when their stories hold together. . . ."

—Ernest Hemingway,
The Sun Also Rises

"... if you try to do something different in this country, people put you down for it."

—Eric Dolphy

"Art never seems to make me peaceful or pure."

—Willem de Kooning

Emergency Exit

Stop: The doorway of life. Take this cliché with ancient roots as a central motif. The practice of carrying the new bride across the threshold stems from a tribal Jewish custom. Its function was complex, full of mystery, and contradictions. A respect for blood (*adom*) as the source of life was at the bottom of it. The tribal Jews were careful not to waste it and considered its loss a sin. Women were creatures who periodically lost, "wasted," blood; therefore, they were born eternally guilty and damned. This male attitude toward the female evolved out of male fear of the mysterious ability of the female to give birth. There were many other male behavior patterns manifested as a result of this anxiety. One theory has it that all male-oriented civilizations evolved from it. Indications of it are not only observable among tribal peoples today but can be seen in the interactions of people in industrialized societies.

Sacred blood had the power to heal and to protect the ancient Jews from evil. The Blood of the Lamb is both real and symbolic. Animal blood was customarily smeared all along the doorway and across the threshold of the Jewish home to keep away evil spirits. As a symbol of goodness and a substance of hope and faith, the ancient Jews practiced this ritual. Because women are eternally guilty of sin they had to be lifted and carried across the threshold and they could not *touch* the doorway. Yet they, the givers of life itself, were the *source* of the symbolism and the ritual. They were the doorway of life.

Some ancient Jews drove their women to the caves in the hills during their cycle as punishment for losing blood. The uterus was perhaps the most mysterious thing among tribal peoples throughout the ancient world. Many other tribes practiced various forms of these rituals of the doorway, the threshold and the cave. Such customs have unmistakable functions and the riddles implicit at their centers attempt to speak to the ultimate mystery of life itself. While women were damned—out of fear—they were at the same time the secret object of the profoundest worship. In many tribal cultures men did not realize they had had any part in the birth process.

Emergency Exit. Standing in the blood on the holy threshold right now are so many friends and enemies I'd be up all night trying to remember their names. I see Jean Valjean, Ernest Hemingway, Camille Dumas. And Alice Carroll. Karenina Tolstoy. David Dickens. Slayer Cooper. Gulliver Swift. Henry Thack. Bigger Thomas. Toomer Cane. Nat Gables. Jim Conrad. Cross Damon. Ted R. Tragicar. Harriet Cabin and Portnoy. Gene Autry, Shirley Temple, Spike Jones, Johnny Carson. Jane Brontë. Holden Caulfield. Enrico Caruso, Nelson Eddy, Stephen Foster, Jelly Roll Morton. Johnny Beetlecreek. Doris Catacombs. Mr. Hamlet. Horatio. Ahab. Mr. Ibsen. Dr. Stockmann. Mr. Babo. Oh, Mr. Babo with his razor. Victor Hunch. Dick Herman. John Pilgrim. Anthony Zenda and Black Michael. Charlie Messenger in his yellow wig. The Invisible Man. Stephen Courage and Dan Robinson. There's Hester Prynne, still wearing the curse. And Nog dragging that thing around. The Ginger Man. Steve Saw finding tiny elephants in an old rusty can. Ishtar from upstate. And Sancho Panza stealing the show from Mr. Don. Helga Crane, neither Black nor white. Van Gogh. The Beatles. Stonewall Jackson. Mr. Allworthy and Tom. And Charles Darnay and Catherine Barkley still saying what a dirty trick it is. And Fred Henry still listening. None of them change. Deruchette Hugo will always be charming. Falstaff and Shylock will remain. Prufrock measures his life. Mrs. Bovary, there in the doorway, cannot get the blood off her underwear. Edmond Dantès counts out his days. Emily Wuther. Charles Ho. H. G. Worlds is still at war. Vivian Grey. Oliver Wake and the Archbishop Thomas Beckett. None of them will ever step away from that spot they occupy on the threshold, their feet stuck in the blood. The Lone Ranger. Raskolnikov. Huck. Walt. King Kong. D. H. It's a crowded place.

Call me Dracaena Messangeana. I don't mind.

"I always knock on wood before I make my entrance."

—Will Rogers,
American Indian

"The threshold of a Mongol's yurt is . . . traditionally a sensitive place that involves taboo. The belief among the common people is that to step on the threshold of a yurt is tantamount to stepping on the neck of the owner . . . there were reports of foreign emissaries being killed for stepping on the threshold of the royal pavilion as they entered and of guards being placed on either side of the door to lift up and carry in foreign emissaries in order to avoid this fate."

—Sechin Jagchid and Paul Hyer,
Mongolia's Culture and Society

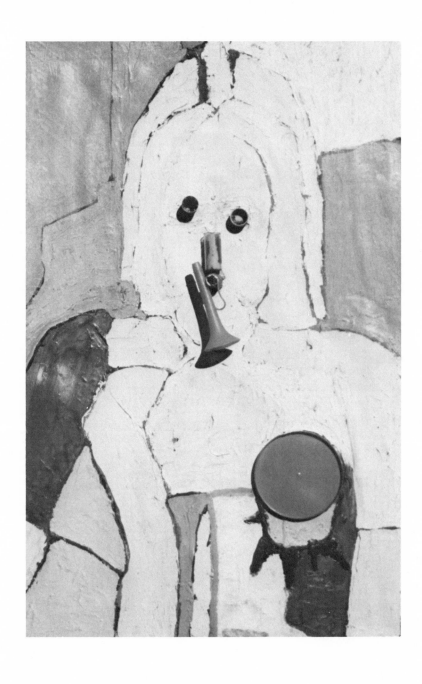

The New (Threshold) Law

In the township of Inlet, Connecticut from this day (February 12, 19—) forward, all males (over the age of 21) will be required to lift from the ground, floor or landing or any flat surface made for standing or walking, leading to a door and/or doorway, all females (over the age of 18) and carry such females through, beyond, out of, said doorways, entranceways, exits, across, beyond, thresholds, of all buildings, dwellings, public and private, taking stern and serious care that no physical part of the bodies of said females touch in any manner whatsoever the physical parts of such entranceways, doorways and exits.

Failure to comply with this ruling of the city government will result in arrest and possible conviction; the nature of punishment will be determined by the Civil Court of Inlet, Connecticut. (Punitive Law Number 1026)

Seal: **Rocky T. Mountain**
                                  Mayor

Witness: *James Russell Ingram*

The sky cleared. The backyard is beautiful. I'm sitting here looking through the window at the trees, five of them, and the sky behind them. A long shadow, thick and dark, made by the house covers most of the yard. The December trees beyond the yard are purple. Quickly I write this: "This tree is green with large black limbs. Touch the tree. The fence is uneven. Black lines enclose it, the nails are rust-covered and showing through the rotten wood. I sit on the ground with my back against a woman's back. We sleep this way. Trucks go by on the road, whistling against the long stretch of lonesome highway. The trees down the road are naked, unbearable. This person that is me is reaching out in contradictions. I want to paint my way out of this. Write my way out. This landscape is not for this tree. Fences like this should be in movies, only. My woman should be home in bed. I should be home in bed with her. These trucks should drive on. Drivers who drive on eventually drive through the beautiful forest where Kenneth Patchen sees blue animals."

We go home and play cards. My woman loves to be inside the house, it is the safest place in the world. We throw cards at each other: The Queen of Spades, Seven of Spades, Nine of Diamonds, Six of Clubs, Queen of Hearts, and Four of Hearts.

A storm comes down into the ocean. About certain other things you can't be sure. Like this: a woman comes into the room with a portable TV. She says it's time for Uncle Walter C. She sits the set on my desk. Says let's watch.

Uncle Walter C. says: Today in Inlet, Connecticut sixty-three women were arrested for refusing to be lifted and carried across the thresholds of public buildings. Hours earlier, these and about a hundred other women staged a protest march in front of Inlet Court House. Inlet, of course, is the town that made international headlines a week ago when it passed a law requiring all men to carry all women across all thresholds at all times. Reporter Jack Pennies talked with the Mayor Rocky T. Mountain this afternoon. Here's his report.

Pennies holds the microphone to the mayor's mouth and the mayor speaks: This law is our attempt to restore moral sanity and honor and dignity to at least this small part of the world! And by god we think we'll win despite those—those *unpleasant* type women out there on the street! We're thinking with this law of the awful failure of marriages, the vanishing family in our society, we're thinking this law will bring back into our lives the kind of stability we all need! Those radical gals out there aren't even aware that this law is for their own good!

Listen: Inlet Research Company reports: purity deep in the psyche racism deep in the psyche cleanliness and proper conduct both deep in the psyche. Facts: Inlet population: eighty-seven point twenty-one percent white, twelve point three percent black, three point seven percent Spanish-speaking and less than one percent other. Fifty percent work in offices handling paper and telephones earning between ten and twenty-five thousand. Eighty percent own cars. Average rent: between one hundred and a hundred and fifty per month many own their own homes. Only nine point seven percent get their hands dirty every day earning less than seven thousand per year. Six percent work at crafts making leather belts. One percent farm. They all own washers dryers dishwashers air conditioners freezers and two percent own second homes. How do you like them apples.

The Ingram family stands quietly on the stone walkway waiting for Jim's trousers to dry in the sunlight the pants are spread out on a brick wall. Old faded temple on other side. They are in another world. Thousands of tiny windows hand carved figures around each Julie is naked Deborah is thin in a thin gown Jim inspects his pants turns them over. Runs his hand into the left leg then the right his eyes are deep the child watches his father in order to know what to do next.

A cowbell rings in the distance. A Monk prays in a temple. Deborah clicks her tongue against the roof of her mouth. She opens her mouth sticks her tongue out at the temple and the cowbell, she stops and Barbara starts crying.

9

The Ingram family has gathered together. Jim sits in the hand carved Jacobean chair Barbara wears a golf ball made of gold around her neck Julie has a Deborah Goldsmith painting of one of her ancestors Deborah sits on a wainscot chair. Barbara has brought her fairy lamp with her Julie is working her embroidery frame Oscar is picking his abscesses with a silver pin Deborah scratches his fissures Barbara has an X-ray of a growth in her bladder. Julie is tinkling with the expensive Coalport and Caughley in Jim's hallway. All the doors all the windows are open. Crooks watch from outside. Everything is insured especially the Chippendale antiques and the canted candlestick holder.

I (your narrator) parked my car on the road went down to say hello to thirty cows eating grass they all came to the fence to greet me. I cut the fence and they stepped across the threshold into the ditch followed me up to the car we went down to the local beer pub and got smashed. The bartender was so delighted he set us up twice. Said all we have to do is vote for his man. I can't remember the guy's name.

Deborah is playing with the ring on her finger. She watches the finger ease up to the opening then she plunges the finger through the ring. She pulls it out with just as much ceremony. It's fun she says her husband continues to look worried it's the same expression he has when he smells something bad like rotten onions.

You finish washing your body and lock the bathroom door. You break down the wall that separates your apartment from the one next to yours. A family is there gathered around a table eating summer food. You dance for them then take up a collection for your services. Under the table surrounded by their feet you sleep dreaming of being lost in one of Goya's paintings.

Julie has turned into an old witch. Sitting on her left shoulder is a demon in the shape of a frog with two horns. The toad whispers into Julie's ear: The researcher is not the one. The frontiersman is not the one. The Black Professor is not the one. Your father's girl friend, Roslyn Carter, is not the one. There is a man whose name is B-sounding with an S-sounding last name who is lusting after you though he has never seen you. Don't see him. Your presence fills his dreams every night. If he were to meet you he'd make you very unhappy. Might even cause your death. Ride your broom and lead a clean life. Think health.

1. In my professional life I am a success. In my amateur life . . . ?

2. You girls are no longer my daughters!

3. I love you but you make me sick sometimes.

4. Your father and I told you what we expect of you . . .

5. I wish you were dead!

6. No child of mine would talk to me like that!

7. Yuk! Look at you!

8. I wish I'd never been born.

9. Oh, gee, I feel so goooood today! Isn't it a wonderful day?

10. I'm tired of office work.

11. Yak yak!

12. You two are going to be the death of me!

13. You didn't think of your mother and me when you were out running around with your friends.

14. What is it that you want—I don't understand you!

15. I wish you'd stop drinking.

16. Would you please listen to me!

17. Hi.

18. I love you when you lift me across the threshold. Oh, darling, I love you soooooo much!

a. I didn't ask to be born.

b. *I hate you, I hate you!*

c. Why can't we be like other families?

d. You never lift me across the threshold.

e. I love you, do you know that . . .

f. Talk to me while we make love, I love to hear you talk to me . . .

g. I feel hysterical. Do I seem crazy. I feel crazy.

h. Go fly a kite!

i. I hate you when you lift me across the threshold. I hate this house, too. And you, too.

19. So what else is new?
20. I just want problems I can handle.
21. Say pretty please.
22. Turn to page two-twenty-two. Everybody sing! Two-twenty-two.
23. I wish I had been born in another time. Say the 20's.
24. Did you look in the attic?
25. You make me sick but I love you. Deep down I always love you.
26. I don't want to talk about it right now. Tomorrow, okay.
27. Look at the mess you've made of your life.
28. Do you work for the CIA?
29. My brother doesn't get to spend enough time with his father. My father is always with his girl friend.
30. Nobody loves me.

j. I don't like the food available in this country. I'm not at home here.
k. Kiss.
l. Love is a pie.
m. Mother where are my paper shoes?

n. I don't like the taste of myself on your mouth and beard when we kiss. I know it's a hangup but I can't help it.

o. Oh, well.
p. Have you seen the painting by Morris Hirschfield (1872–1946) called "Nude on Sofa with Three Pussies"? Quite an accomplishment!
q. She's depressed. I hope she doesn't kill herself.

"There is a serious gap between our ideals and some of our practices . . ."

—President Truman

"Backdoor Spending: a term used by opponents of the policy of financing a federal program without going through the normal procedure of making an appropriation. . . ."

—Eugene J. McCarthy,
Dictionary of American Politics

"We keep a horse in the house. Just an old broken down hack we picked up in New Hampshire when I play the piano it tries to tap dance. Thinks he's human." *UPI—Horse kept in house bumps head on kitchen doorway while entering dining room.*

My wife (the narrator's wife) digs in the hillsides for ancient cities she always wears a red raincoat so hunters won't shoot her. Last year she slid down into a mudhole and found herself standing on the tomb of a king who lived six thousand years ago.

The new apartment is full of empty milk cartons Julie walks around naked all day pressing the kittens to her breasts.

Column one page one: husbands *must* carry wives across thresholds through doors maximum penalty for violators.

This cave in the earth is endless. Things warm with tense muscles hide for years in it. The darkness is a darkness full of change. I eat the sunlight drink the sea sunk in it I digest the earth swim deep in my own nervous system, here inside I listen to the pounding of the heart, this strange thing, that surrounds me. I sleep and wake in the blackness and change in it when the beating rhythm changes. It changes when the seasons change which changes when the cave itself changes.

Houses are built the wrong way the walls do not feel like skin or hair. The people in them keep trying to rebuild themselves from scratch. Scraps of ideas won't work.

A threshold is a sill some dwellers think of a threshold as a doorway in fact it is the sill of a doorway the entrance to the house a holy holy place beginning blood of the lamb guilt the exit the whole thing all over again, again and again.

This living thing hides from the light and drinks little water.

This is a place of inletting where rock stars easily make up songs about one's state of . . . when one is let in on the ultimate secret of the "limen" the "threschold" the "traskvald" the "threscwald" the . . .

Jim and Deborah are standing in the yard together. Her hair is parted down the middle. The expensive rings he gave her are on the fingers of the left hand. Held against her long black dress they shine.

Jim protects me like a father Deborah says. He wears his long grey locks over his ears and down his neck. Sad angry eyes.

The corner of Roslyn's mouth twitches.

Deborah's sister Alla Blake is visiting them at the moment she's jumping from the diving board into the swimming pool she's achieved a fine tan the pink and green of her swimsuit against her body is beautiful. When she dives with both arms up her hair hugs her neck she plunges into the sky.

Sixteen persons at Inlet are listed in *Who's Who in America* but the best known is a short story writer who publishes in New York two of his best known stories are, "Think Health: Eat Your Honey!" and "It Takes Balls to Play

Tennis." In the first an old woman carries a horse and buggy across the threshold of a barn—this is all she ever does. In the second a weak dirty man learns how to be strong and hygienic. The other sixty writers in town are unpublished and unknown they get together and exchange rejection slips.

Barry Sands walks into the room. Julie is sitting at the desk reading. He sneaks up behind her and places his hands over her eyes. Guess who. I can't. I'm your hypnotist, he says. He releases her eyes. Look into my eyes. She turns and looks up into his eyes. Repeat after me. I will always hold a raw potato in my mouth while peeling onions. Julie repeats the words though they mean nothing to her. Barry continues: I am a rabbit who will eventually lay an egg. He listens carefully as she repeats it. I will fall in love with a handsome young Jewish man and live happily ever after. Rather than repeating Barry's word Julie—as though another's voice is speaking through her—says: Pax sax sarax afra afca nostra.

They are bike riding along the path in Central Park
and stop and put down the bikes and stretch out on the
grass avoiding dog turds. Looking then at the sky Julie
speaks in a phony voice. I hope someday you and I can go
to Africa together. You'd love Africa, Al. You would like to
wouldn't you. He laughs. Certainly. Tries to say certainly
like proper people. Sometimes he felt she was simply
flaunting the fact that she'd been to Africa twice once as a
little girl then later to attend college. Rich niggers from
Inlet, Connecticut, going to see the savages no that's not the
right image. Returning to one's homeland but Julie Al
thinks doesn't see Africa that way. Roots. Boots. Ah so
what. Africa might be a place you could dig after all even
after Tarzan and white lies. Little white lies. Hello white
lies. White lies uneasily on the canvas. Oh it would be so
great to see Africa with you Al! She closes her eyes and sees
the rolling green hills and the warm storms the rains high
in the mountains. Feels herself moving along the street of
an East African country the warmth in her African
garments. Dark people standing in doorways watching. Al
and Julie now on their backs side by side. You know the
more I think about it Al says the more appealing the idea is.
You mean seeing Africa with me. Yes. She suddenly sat up
and threw herself over on him hugging him and kissing his
face all over. Over and over. It annoyed him her dramatics
but at this point he could live with them her way. Today was
Friday and tonight they were going to Inlet to spend the
weekend together in Julie's parents' home in Duck Pond
while Jim and Deborah were away together on a cruise
trying to patch up but not really patch up their cracked
marriage. Julie's parents had asked her not to have her

boyfriends stay all night while they were away but she was going to do it anyway because this time it was different since Allen Morris was the man she'd spend the rest of her life with. An all night visitor was another matter but Al was special. If mom and dad found out they would understand they would have to understand. They'd have the house to themselves. Hello house. Nice and warm inside the word house. Deep inside the house they would plunge deep inside each other. All the way back. They'd have the whole house except perhaps for Barbara who might return home from visiting her best friend a white girl named Nikki. But so what they'd still have privacy and Julie was happy. To her Al looked happy too.

They ride the bikes back to the rental place. On the way Al leads the way through a tunnel. Inside the tunnel an eye follows them. The eye has a voice it says: mirror mirror. Al says huh and Julie says I didn't say anything.

They went to Julie's apartment in the city and fucked but they also made love with each other after fucking became a bore. Julie's next door neighbors an old man on one side an old woman on the other always listened through the walls. Julie and Al were aware of this and enjoyed being the objects of such interest. One day in the hall the old woman stood in front of Julie's door. She had a huge purse. She was an old woman who fished around in her purse for a match and she had gone forty-eight days without finding one. In the beginning the dog had been with her but since her luck had gone bad the dog died of starvation and now she was alone with her purse and her bad luck. Julie felt sorry for old folks. She wanted to rub their backs and cook dinner for them but she couldn't take care of every old person in the world. The word world was too big. She had to draw the line somewhere so she drew it at the point before a start becomes possible.

It was all right to make love for a long time because they were waiting for the rush hours to pass before going to the train station.

They took the seven forty-seven and when they got there they climbed in a taxi driven by a resentful white guy with a big head giving them dirty racist looks in the rearview mirror.

Before the train pulled out it scratched its confused brow. A naked woman was running trying to catch it.

Within minutes they reached the Ingram home a white house with green lawn and trimmings on a tree-lined street and inside always inside the living room was soft like flesh subdued colors and from it you could see the dining room and its staid furniture hard thick and cool and going in the other direction the entrance to the ultramodern kitchen white and gold and yellow and green and a stairway both to the basement and going up to the deep secrets of the bedrooms like the insides of living creatures that have lived longer than time. All very plush and immediately Julie places a record on the stereo. *Axis: Bold as Love / The Jimi Hendrix Experience.* Side One *Up From The Skies.* Up full blast through the house with just the two of them together deep inside the secure place. Oh how she had always wanted it to be this way. So romantic and cozy with the whole world way away outside. Here in her parents house she always wanted to do it in their bed. Imagine doing it actually having sex making out in dad's bed. At last. The risk was great and this was the chance. Mom and dad. Jiggs and Maggie. Dagwood and Blondie. Dale Evans and Roy Rogers.

Yes the risk. Barbara might return resentful overweight Barbara just might burst into the room.

Meanwhile darkness moved all around the house. The word dark cannot explain just how dark it was how quiet how peaceful. It was a darkness bought with impressive money. Say Money . . . Barbra Streisand owned a house down the block. Dick Tracy lived two blocks over. Dr. Spock ran a clinic five minutes from here. Norman Mailer spent his summers in a house nearby.

As darkness moved around the house like a hand around a wine glass Julie poured wine into two glasses. They sipped the stuff from sparkling orange glasses. The dry red wine was just right it warmed the belly. Al closed his eyes. Inside his head he saw a row of sheep houses lining the north west countryside. How did sheep or people live in houses.

As though reading his thoughts Julie said Winston Churchill once lived in a house.

So did Harpo Marx.

And Brenda Starr. She lived in an apartment didn't she.

I think so. Booker T. Washington also spent a lot of time inside.

Inside what.

Houses. We're talking houses aren't we. Say. Abe Lincoln too. And Walter Cronkite and Adolf Hitler and even Snoopy. Snoopy has a house.

There's an actress who lives in our neighborhood. She lives in the green house at the corner.

Who is she?

Never heard of her.

Janice Page is going with Barry Sands. That's a rumor. They don't live in the same house. Some characters those two.

Tell me more Julie.

I assume all these houses have doors.

And windows.

As darkness continued to move around the house Al felt a long way from home the strangeness of being way out here at night in a strange house with a girl who was suddenly strange.

When Barbara came in they were still on the living room floor drinking wine and kissing and speaking and touching sensitive areas of each others bodies. Barbara quickly looked away saying hello while quickly walking through. They heard her slam her bedroom door.

Al had not told Julie that he and Barbara had once had sex together two summers ago to be exact. He now suspected that Barbara loved him or something otherwise why was she so hostile.

Ah shit no fucking in mom's bed tonight but there's tomorrow. She's mad about something and when Barbara is mad like that she'll tell our parents anything to get them pissed off so I'll have to get angry too. She wants the whole fucking world to be miserable with her. If she'd lose weight she wouldn't be so unhappy she could keep a boyfriend.

They went up on tiptoes to Julie's bedroom and before sleep they had a wild sweaty lusty love struggle that released them from tension then they slept going into stage one sleep. Julie sank to stage two where she was operating the light on a lighthouse. The sky is big and clean and innocent. Al stayed at stage one. Julie dropped down to stage three where she could not dream anything. Deep into the night she was floating around outside herself in stage four. Al remained in stage one. There at stage one he found himself chained to a large platform controlled by tiny workmen. They were pushing dead birds into his mouth.

In the morning Barbara's face was swollen from crying half the night. Red eyes a dry tight mouth.

The three of them sipped coffee together at the small table in the kitchen.

Al sat beside Barbara facing the narrow kitchen window. Through it he gazed at the lighthouse. At its base a giant bird with the head of a monk was eating a naked man. He yawned. Julie's back was to the window and she yawned too.

Around eleven Barbara announced that she was going boating with friends.

She left wearing tight shorts and tennis shoes.

Julie and Al looked at each other.

Suck me, he said.

This realism is my darkest light. A purple light glowing in the dark. Ain't nothing like it no where nothing never in life like it, nothing *this* good: it is the only thing; nothing better conceivable! Deep way down low where the energy really counts. At the edge of

himself. He was a man huge and brutal. Believed in himself and even if he was a character you still had to deal with the reality of him as character. Call him Hal call him Ron Barry Dick Al. Call him your best friend yourself.

Threading and frilling through tides of . . . an unbroken perfect rhythm. Tossing and turning. Every moment. But how could he be so given to good luck. Good luck yall.

Hi I'll try to be sane again. Nobody on earth was this lucky. All the Inlet characters were not this lucky. They had to wash dishes take out the garbage. Sleep. Snore. Things other people do. But they could not grow old could not change, attitudes toward them could change but they would never change. He was the single exception: a character who COULD change but did he change that is the question. His luck said he could do anything he wanted to do. Do it do it do it, as many times as he wanted to do it. He made the name stick. Feel right inside his body, inside his body's body, inside the body of his mind, deep inside his *his*.

Working on a train . . . No, I take that back. Never did he work on a train. He was himself a piston a sort of precision. Listening to the grunts and whispers and speeches in parks and painful pleasure and he was a delighted *being*. Enough time.

Then he met a woman. Stella Cora Rea Cindy Julie

Barbara Deborah Gertrude Janice Sandy Marcia Sharon Cynthia Nikki Christer Gail Rose Marie Gloria Alla, you name her. He met her. He knew her she whispered in his ear you are a beautiful person. So beautiful in fact I would die for your beauty.

Well he didn't lose control of himself he kept his head and kept right on.

From the semidark beginning to the shuddering ends of themselves they kept meeting. They got together in this world and held their sponginess together; touched their sweetness, their eyes opened pulling the outlines of themselves into a oneness.

He lifts her and she lifts him. They even have time to reflect on the wet outline of their own delight. Wide dark and deep. This realism is their darkness so powerful it lasts for the rest of . . .

A quality that seems to go on. He's this way and she's that way. His stomach grumbles her nerves are kicked raw. Hey! a moment of rest! Her face turns his face turns. Inside outside. Go easy go fast. His saliva is in the palm of his hands and it is the beginning of work, hard work.

The goodness of Life nearly left him. The work was deadening, thankless, dull, shit. He lost himself in it and its timeclocks and stinginess, smallness, meanness. Could it really be in America the land of the free and the home of the nervous the land of milk and rice the melting pan the . . ?

She held on to him with her love but love did not save him from a private ache in the brain.

"Just think survival."

And she held on to him. He was the man more than his fingers or eyes suggested and she this woman you see so lovely so strong did not believe in equal rights for women because, as she said, it meant equal responsibility she felt her place, as she explains it, "is *behind* my man," and there he was, broken, crawling through credit cards, Sears catalogues, babyshit, Kenmore washers, hope.

The pain of moving around inside yourself and the pleasure of moving throughout yourself. Try to be easy and natural, you are easy and natural.

Then suddenly they won the lottery and the million changed their lives—their life?

They can slide the objects around rearrange them for a deeper truer vision of the experience. She takes a deep breath. At times it's more fun than you can ever imagine: having your cake and the money too.

The red and blues and yellows are beautiful around them. But the smart woman begins to see her dumbness and there is an ache in her head she must come to terms with. A scream of pleasure in the middle of madness and night does not release her. Nothing suddenly begins you know. You also know . . . or *think* you know that suddenly nothing ends suddenly.

Everything comes together in a novel—life is another matter. Even when a composition by the woman and the man is apparently working against conventional composition, with their luck, and the good spirits of Inlet, it comes together. Ain't nothing on earth nearly half as beautiful. Let it continue. The last of the moments. The first of the slow middle. Let it all continue!

An old wool blanket covers Jim's otherwise naked body. His pipe smoke drifts up where the sunlight from the window splits it.

They arrested Barbara for shitting on a public threshold. The judge said she should be sent "to the back of the cave." Endless Summer was her nickname.

They oil the robot. It walks to the door. Looks out. Smiles.

Patrick and Rose Marie hide in the basement eating peanuts and leaving their fingerprints in the dust.

Deborah stretches out the length of a parking lot. She is waiting for anything.

The ocean beats its arms against the rocks two boys Patrick and Oscar are down at the beach trying to push a raft out the sand where the boys stand is still dark gold in late moonlight. The boys are careful not to speak.

The Ingram family is entering a place where words are not useful where grown men stand in doorways of jets and ships and wave to dead wives. And cameras. The ocean has a bad attitude when it slaps the face of the land. It's hot the heat comes in cold waves. I open my mouth it enters, the heat swells while I run I am dreaming I am falling flying out of a bat cave, trying to rediscover the ship the ocean the aircraft the people I saw standing there, nice people, simply waving goodbye. I am both relieved and astonished that none of this ever happened till now.

A translator who ate nothing but fish died.

Three men and two women were arrested last night for killing pigs and chickens in an apartment in downtown Inlet.

A young woman named Cindy who taught breast feeding your infant at the college was suspended for breast feeding her own infant in class. They locked her out and threw away the infant.

There's a war going on so you see a lot of soldiers walking around without arms and real legs.

That girl Rosetta I told you about still wears her mother's raspberry ribbon and sings in the shower of her abortions, dreams and . . .

Old people spend the day on the phone talking to other old people, there is a connection, a quiet, almost silent, underground connection . . .

Rose Marie, fed up, went to the supermarket naked and climbed into a Time Clock where the workers punch out.

Those husbands and fathers who do not carry their women-folk across thresholds may be revolutionaries.

Saturday Elmer Blake went down to his car in the garage and found the engine ripped to pieces the hair of an animal was all over it.

The sun does not go deep into the ocean.

The skin torn at the edges of love heals very quickly.

Grown men dressed as women in high heels strut about in their tiny rooms to understand what happened . . .

"Too much honey turns sour in the fat stomach. It is wise to give in to your fate. Rats under the skin don't necessarily mean you are having a nightmare."

Barry Sands is driving along a dark country road outside Inlet. He crosses an old bridge. Just as he reaches the other side the bridge collapses. The old man who lives beneath it manages to crawl from beneath the rubble. He shakes his fist at Barry's vanishing car. Just as sure as my name is Obeah I will get even with you! I will cast a spell that will keep Julie out of your reach forever!

"Bess or Betty: housebreakers use this instrument to open doors. Goes back to England, 1811."

"Emergency #8, Car in Water. (You may miss a turn on an unfamiliar road and drive into a lake, or an old country bridge may collapse and send your car into the water.)
1. Remember that many cars float for 5 or 6 minutes.
2. Try to escape from the car through a window rather than a door . . .
3. If you cannot escape before the car sinks, take several deep breaths and ride car to bottom . . . Take a few deep breaths and try a door which can now be opened since inside and outside pressures are now equalized, or roll down a window. It is not advisable to try and open a door while sinking because the pressure of the onrushing water could crush you."

> —Seymour Weiser,
> *Emergency Situations in Driving*
> The Automobile Club of America, Inc.

"door (dór, dôr), n. 1. a movable, usually solid barrier for opening and closing an entranceway, cupboard, cabinet, or the like, commonly swinging on hinges or sliding in grooves. 2. a doorway. 3. the building, house, etc., to which a door belongs: *two doors down the street.* 4. any means of approach, access, or exit: the doors to learning. 5. lay at someone's door, to hold someone accountable for: *We laid the blame for the mistake at his door.* 6. out of doors, outside of buildings; in the open: *We couldn't wait to get out of doors again after the long winter.* 7. show someone the door, to request or order someone to leave. [ME *dore,* OE *duru* door, *dor* gate; akin to G *Tür,* Icel *dyrr,* Gk *thyra,* L *foris,* etc.]"

—Laurence Urdang,
Stuart Berg Flexner,
The Random House Dictionary of the English Language

Every time we turn around we are here again: a large sea-side house. Sad shadows beneath window ledges doorways under the roofing of the porch along its sides under and behind the trimmings drain pipes along the sides under the house itself.

The windows are still damp from a recent hard rain roof porch soggy mosquitos drift along floorboards nobody's here the flagpole juts out from the top casting a long lonely shadow nobody's inside there is a stillness.

Julie's sleeping right now.

On the pier the boat turned over to dry in the sun. Sunlight falls straight down on rooftops.

The wharf runs along to the shore along it houses filled with ropes and harpoon tackle. Harpooners hang out in nearby taverns drinking ale.

Harpsichord music comes from Jim Ingram's anchored yacht a harpist is in love with the girl from Harper's Ferry the harp players in town are all in for the night.

Right now Deborah couldn't care less. She's sleeping on the beach.

Children are combing the beach for shells. Exotic birds nearby squawking, trying to feed their young. They guard their space. The mouths of the young gape.

Farmers in the rain holding umbrellas over their own heads standing at the rear of a row of dairy cows. At the fence Jim watches. He has money invested in these animals and their caretakers!

Julie and Barbara are on the beach clowning. One in red pants the other in yellow. Chasing each other around, playing tag. Julie catches Barbara and throws her down rolls her in the sand.

We're on a hillside sunk in tall grass. My head on her lap. "You're beautiful, Dreamy, the most beautiful woman."

I feel the pains coming now in large and larger waves looping and enclosing me. My large white hat falls into the valley. Wind chasing it downhill. The city below is covered with a halo of smog.

"We will raise our child in the church there are nearly three billion non-Christians in the world I feel sorry for them they are missing the point." "Yes dear."

Jim's eyes are bloodshot. His white jacket is stained with his own lack of professional concern. The woman is naked, white as paper, and fat. Thick masses of veins in her oddly shaped breasts and thighs, a sagging belly. Soft long curly pubic hair between bulging thighs. She steps down from the examination table. Above his head, in his imagination, Jim makes love to her. His secretary walks in and screams. A draft slams the door.

Who called while I was out? Benny Gilford Aaron Giesow Chester Doherty Sam Dogan Isabel Colon Raymond Harris Max Jones Victor Harrison Clarence Snow Herman Goldberg Ann Gold Patricia Grove. And Joan Prado.

Barry Sands is dreaming: he's making love to a beautiful colored girl named Julie Ingram. At the point of orgasm Julie turns into Janice Page a white woman and Barry loses his erection. In his next dream he is being hung by a black hangman. When the stool is kicked from beneath Barry's feet and his neck breaks his penis becomes erect again.

Absentmindedly Deborah picks up her mother's Bible which hasn't been opened in years. She is stunned by what she reads: "if a man shall lie with a woman having her sickness, and shall uncover her nakedness; he hath discovered her fountain, and she hath uncovered the fountain of her blood: and both of them shall be cut off from among their people. *Leviticus,* 20:18." *Shit!* says Deborah. She throws the old book in a corner and immediately decides to go sailing.

Julie answers the phone it's Barry Sands he wants to speak to Herbie Hancock you have the wrong number she tells him.

Janice answers the phone it's Jim Russell Ingram he wants to speak to Nixon is this Mrs. Nixon no you've got the wrong . . .

Jack Pennies answers the phone it's Oscar Wilde he wants to speak to John Keats he tells him he has the wrong century.

Sandy answers the phone it's Barbara she wants to speak to P. P. who? Just P. Sorry, wrong number.

The phone rings in the Glans Removal Shop and it's Joe Smith he wants to speak to Leo. No Leo here. Cancer but no Leo.

Hourari answers his phone it's Jomo he wants to speak to Julie sorry no Julie here who are you any way.

Rose Marie answers the phone it's Stella and Rose Marie wants Albert or was it Phillip she can't remember but he has a heavy voice and she'd know it if she heard it. Stella tells her to kiss off.

Anki answers the phone it's Fish he wants to speak to Slick but there's no Slick in Anki's home. She hangs up.

Bob answers the phone it's Jim who says Sorry Bob I thought I was dialing Rosetta's number. See you.

S. calls B. and B. doesn't live there any more. The number is correct but it's Joe Louis's number. He tells her he doesn't mind she can call again no problem.

Gail answers the phone it is Rea Rea says Listen I got this great story to tell you and Gail says what number do you want and Rea says isn't this Dick no it's not Dick and Gail hangs up.

Barry answers the phone and it's Cindy who wants to speak to Patricia there's no Patricia here what the hell is going on.

Frank Hannigan answers his phone and it's Pete *and* Sam and they want to to know what time they should show up for work tomorrow Frank says is this supposed to be an obscene call or something.

The phone rings in the Mayor's office it's Lord Byron he wants to know about Freud whether or not he should rewrite his stuff the Mayor says you have the wrong number but vote for me anyway.

The phone rings in the Mayor's office his secretary answers and says the Mayor never answers his own phone can I help you yes says the voice—it's Stella Della—tell him our date is off so the secretary tells the strumpet, Stella Della, she has the wrong number.

Levine called a secret number and Robin answered and said Who there's no Marcia here you must have the wrong number. Levine said I'm sorry.

Johnny Hawkins answered the phone in his dressing room and it was She. Listen She he said I'm due on stage in five minutes. I don't know you but after the show I'm willing to do something about it. How about you?

Jim and Deborah and Al and Julie and Barbara and Nikki and Gail and everybody else you can imagine are trying to get in The Place before the Door closes. It is difficult to get tickets. You have to apply months in advance. There is a long line waiting. On line behind them are Cindy and Hal, Stella and Ron, Rea and Dick. There's Janice Page, Charles of Dixie. Trudy Douglas. You know Trudy, don't you? Harpo Marx. Booker T. and Adolph. There's Miss Barbara S. and Dagwood and Jiggs. Jim is clearly impatient. Al feels out of place. Look at his eyes. He looks like a nigger in a white man's blackface show.

You know the painters you met at my house? They all live here in town. One is very well known outside the area. The one who does the Absolute Threshold over and over has no name beyond the state highway out there. Eh? When asked what it means she says it's the level of stimulus required for her sense of herself to rise, to surface. One of the others paints a thing she calls The Gateway of Life. The final one spends most of his time doing himself standing in the doorway of his home. They smoke grass while they work and in most of their paintings you can see smoke.

"I like old men with solid firm eyes. White beards. Red jackets and purple pants. They look good. Their zippers work. They work on the docks. They like to fish. The little bird feet at the edges of their eyes are friendly. Their eyes are doorways to a whole beautiful world of friendliness. They keep their beards trimmed and when they eat they do not drop food on their lovely beards. Some of them wear hearing aids. Those who do not tend to talk more. I watch their mouths as they speak."

Just inside Johnny Hawkins's doorway they grabbed him. The fat man in the straw hat searched Johnny's pants legs for weapons. He spat at them, the fat one and one I didn't mention yet. This other one was going through Johnny's pockets. They found no weapons on Johnny so they let him go. They kicked him and slapped him and told him to be good.

Alla Blake sat rocking in her rocker just inside where the sunlight made the sign of the cross. To her left in her showroom stood a lovely old walnut sleigh bed just for short naps. It was covered with an orange yellow quilt made by a slave who died a slave. A walnut ottoman next to it. A captain's chair complete with handgrips. A blue cat asleep on it. On the wall a reproduction of a Tanner called The Banjo Lesson. When you look at it you can hear the banjo.

Inleters' lips were sealed and their stable doors locked. Others ate grapes of pain and slept in deep beds.

The Ingram kids hide in closets under beds under houses in bushes in abandoned school buses crashed airplanes in the rubbish of vacant lots whispering to each other. They put feathers in their caps and avoided the first blush and persons prone to attic wit and then they could walk   as the crow flies. None of this was original.

Dimestore curtains hang at the Ingram windows facing the road.

The store owner is holding a rusty set of ice tongs. The last customer left an hour ago. He was Jim Ingram who collects antiques.

At lunchtime some workers of Inlet share sandwiches pickles and beer in the doorway of a trailer.

Roslyn Carter knocks on wood and says, Jim you do the same. Jim who is sitting at Roslyn's round table across from her follows her lead and knocks on the table top. What good will this do he wants to know. It will uncross our luck. I'll drink to that. They click wine glasses.

Barry Sands clipped an ad from a newspaper and stuck it in his wallet.

Jim Ingram remembers the beginning of his career. He is proud —and disappointed

Employees wanted: Central Intelligence Agency: An Equal Opportunity Employer. Professional opportunity in many areas. Some new thresholds to be crossed. Send resume to Langley, Virginia.

Janice Page to Barry Sands: "If old women in black lace are selling lace, what is the rest of the story?"

"Dog vomit."

"Don't be a smart ass. Listen, in your protective inner self you are always trying to blunt the equipment of human stammering, hoping that love, money, anything, will then be possible, but what you don't realize is a close relationship with someone like me involves many things: myself as one of two young women pissing on a diamond-studded doorway in City Hall; yes, even old women selling woven and knitted things from their low stools; and when you ask me to meet you at your place you have to understand that we might sleep together, really sleep together and not fuck. Because if you can't understand this propaganda as art then your erection is a sham, a silly little tool, a flash in the pan."

In due time, Barry's response: "All right. No more dog vomit. But what about the old men who marry girls; what about people who lock themselves in their homes because *something dangerous* is out there; what about my relatives who go down to the inlet to watch the tiny paper boats arrive from the land of No; what about ugly girls who can't get rid of walls between themselves and lighted backrooms, whimpering old men, New York, isolated country roads with rich girls speeding along them without lights at night; what about all this? What about the pubic hair, all the pubic hair in the world? If you think I am a pig, then tell me why you, too, grunt so often?"

Selfish question, thought Janice. Very selfish.

Barry did not wait for an answer. He was hot, like a character in deterministic fiction of the 1930's, he beats his fists against the table. "Small shabby Indian children are chasing a drunk man on the beach! Why?"

Selfish, selfish.

"Why?" he insists. "Why is my face dark and handsome and why is our relationship in trouble, why why am I yelling, why, why does the possibility of love close up so quietly and jab its dull blade into the soft heartmeat, why?"

"Because everything has happened before. Remember the summer people looked out of windows down on the heads of civil rights marchers, remember robots lifting ladies across thresholds, remember I am one of the two girls on the beach clowning. The one in red pants. The other, the one in yellow, is my sister. I lie. She's my cousin. I lie. She's my friend. I wish she was my older sister. We are chasing the ball. No, we're chasing the dog. I'm the blond. She's the redhead. I am the innocent little girl who goes crazy one morning at the breakfast table, yelling obscene words."

Barry examines the palm of his hand. "Julie—I *mean* Janice . . ."

"Exposed to the aphrodisiac of loneliness, during episodes of puppy love, I had the cruel hand of a boy in my confused body, probing at the center of my lipstick-coated ego long before I realized any of this," Janice said with profound sadness, "long before I laughed, long before I knew *everything* had happened before."

He closed his eyes listening to her voice. There against the skin of his lids were two images of Julie Ingram. Who was this bewitching dark woman always making her presence felt under his skin?

Barry was unsure. He remembered that his mother and father, Ruth and John, were having tea in the garden. By now their bodies were probably quivering beneath their clothes.

Janice started yelling. She was crying. Her words came in spurts, "The inner walls of self stood . . . stood firmly against . . . the morbid lust . . . of pigs . . . and false philosophers."

"I've lost you." He laughed. "May I see you again?"

"My soul moved among old women selling lace. A man at a piano in a large living room, quietly crying."

"The light bulb," said Barry, "the light bulbs inside the barbershop sign burned out last week."

"Won't you ever understand? When you ask to see me again you are conjuring up candlelight, dry white wine, baked salmon."

"My name is Charles Chest."

The desired effect, laughter, is achieved. But Janice ended the laugh with a frozen face, her eyes going from here to there and back again. "Barry what would you say if I told you I'm secretly working in a topless joint where ladies hang out in doorways soliciting vulgar men?"

"Hi ho. Do it again."

"Self-centered bastard." Janice bit off her fingernail. She chewed it, swallowed it. "Let's go to Ned's Eatery."

"At Ned's Salvation Army broads sing Christmas songs. I can't stand the joint, especially this time of year."

"Night life in this city is for the bats."

Barry got down off the fence and stretched his arms above his head. Yawning.

With Barry, Janice thinks, it may never be possible to know a kind of disposition of human victory and in the same instant taste the openings, the only scorned luck a romantic woman, bitch or butch, can lay her claim near. No, he probably isn't the one to trot near the sacred fantasy, the prince. His bottom lip hangs and he is slightly stooped. He's closer to the frog.

He looked at Janice turn around. She was looking up the hill at the graveyard. He watched the way her ass spread out along the fence. Those tight jeans always turned him on.

I follow myself across selected landscapes where the self searches for the fullness of the self. Janice.

"What are you thinking?" He didn't expect an answer.

She looked at his nose. "Mosquitos. Thinking about

mosquitos and how they drift along floorboards; about going out with you and not going out with you; about fucking; about propaganda and the darkness around the doorway; how the word spreads; about how they found the killer sleeping in the sauna; about the self; about you, yes, you and your inability to see the soft lace of old women who have survived, out-survived their oppressors; and yes, about everything . . ."

Gail has the idea of a baby in her body somewhere it sort of floats around unsure of its position, two babies perhaps three.

Julie could not believe her face it fell so loosely against the mirror looking like her mother one tight line for each eye. Her mouth was a blind stroke moving off, an unfinished streak of lightning. She hung there stunned watching the kids outside playing stickball yelling at each other.

I offer mass for the dead. You don't say. My grandparents helped build the thresholds of this city. The post office. The general store. The supermarket. The bank. My great grandfather was the only man successful in altering the conflict between Catholics and Protestants. That's why this place ain't a ghost town today. What's today?

Deborah's belly is protruding she sits half-dressed. The room is small and dingy. A well-dressed man of fifty sits in a chair by the window smoking a thick, expensive cigar. The woman's hair is rolled up to keep her from having to untangle it after a romp. Her pubic hair is thick and black, veins in her ass along her thighs large varicose veins purple in the lamplight. The man looks out the oriel window a slight yellow glimmer of sunrise along the skyline. He takes off his jacket his suspenders are pale red with gold stripes. He strokes his moustache. Deborah slaps her naked belly and laughs. Gotta lose weight.

That same group of young women three black and one yellow two white one red, stand close together, just like before, smelling each other's breath. They blow then they cover their mouths and laugh. They're together under a large loose veil. An owl, with large yellow eyes, flies suddenly into them saying hoo hoo hoo. One screams my god what is that! The screamer is Julie.

I see blood here I am in myself.

There's a woman down there in the river scrubbing two small children. She runs her fingers deep into their ears, cleaning them. The mud at the bottom of the river is warm and it feels good to her feet it has sucked her in a little. It keeps sucking her down. Deborah watches from the bank. I'm lucky she thinks.

Barbara works in the department store. She is counting the underwear and dresses these things people will slide into to feel warm. Deep inside clothes there is a sense of privacy. It's dark in them like an underground city.

A neighbor woman who was sick in bed had her husband throw out the medicine. The dog sleeping at the foot kept whimpering in its sleep. The potchair in the corner smells awful. The windows and doors are locked. There is no fresh air. She is groaning.

Julie steps lightly across cool rocks in the surf stopping to collect bright stones. Her barefeet are pink and gray like the stones. In her womb she feels the separate life moving giving expression to itself. Is she pregnant?

I wrestle gently with abstract news items: people by the thousands are taking to the streets of the cities dancing and fighting teasing wrestling and loving each other. Many are drunk and giant insects and large birds and fish out of water have joined in. There is nothing large enough to contain their excitement. A giant bird with a container clamped in its beak tried this but it didn't work.

Julie goes to the Corked Pussy Cat to apply for a job as waitress. They give her their standard application to fill out. In the lead paragraph she comes across this sentence: persons applying for work at the Corked Pussy Cat should be broken down by age and sex. Julie looks up. Huh?

As daylight fades Jim Ingram and Deborah Ingram arrive. Jim in short sleeves red pullover and yellow pin-striped short pants. White lowcut tennis shoes. He runs his fingers through his silky white hair. Deborah is dressed the same way.

Deborah felt her face stretch. Al, she said, we didn't know you'd be here. Welcome. Did you arrive today?

He looked at Julie. We came last night, Mom.

Deborah's eyes stretched. Oh?

Julie turned down the record player.

Jim said, Is Barb around?

She went sailing.

Deborah's face relaxed. So Barb came last night, too? Yes.

After supper and several drinks out in the back yard Jim says to Al, Julie tells me you and she are very serious about each other.

Yes. Al was being cautious. His hands felt wet. Yellow niggers made him nervous. Well, except Julie.

Julie leaned forward in her redwood chair. But we don't plan to marry—we don't believe in it. It destroys everything. We don't want to go that route. If and when we have children I'll simply have them in my own name.

Jim did not respond he looked at his soft white hands. Then at a fly on the arm of his chair.

Deborah smiled sympathetically, Julie, she said, why don't you show Al our movies from Africa.

Julie smiled. Mom had successfully changed the subject. Good old mom.

The footage is typical homemovie stuff with blind

spots poor dollying unfocused closeups. Silent. Color. Julie is leading a pony around by its bridle. Here she looks like a little white girl. The animal is dark brown with a white streak down its face. Holding on for dear life on the back of the pony are two African children. Here Julie is trying to get baby Barbara to stand alone and walk but Barbara keeps sitting down on the ground. Deborah is helping. One short scene of Julie being bossy lining up a group of African kids and marching back and forth in front of them like a general on an inspection tour. Now a cozy interior scene showing Deborah shapely and lovely playing with both her girls, Oscar her son not born yet. Now a shot of Oscar at birth. Born in Nairobi when it was still a British crown colony.

Sometimes I really miss Kenya, said Deborah. The people there are so beautiful.

What'd you do in Africa? Al asked—of no one in particular. I know Julie was in school there but that was later wasn't it; were you on vacation?

Jim answered. I worked for the American Information Service.

Oh. It meant nothing to Al. Just another bigshot nigger making it in the white world.

More footage. Jim obviously the cameraman makes only one appearance and it is aboard a large pleasure cruiser far out into the Gulf of Guinea during a vacation the family took to West Africa. Other footage from this time shows Julie and Deborah swimming in the Gambia River.

Julie took Al's hand. We were there when Kenyatta took over in '64. He held me on his lap once.

The film is being run backwards now. Julie likes to do this. It thrills her to see figures stepping back rather than forward coming apart rather than together.

Al wets his lip and rests his arm along the backside of the couch. Julie is on the floor in front of him resting her back against his knees.

There's Jim in the film again on the cruiser. He looks younger naturally and taller and thinner and sunburned like a well-to-do white man. In fact in the film he looks whiter than in real life.

The footage ends and Al says, Hey that was nice. He smiles.

Deborah watches him closely. She likes to see him smile. It warms her in secret places.

Julie throws her head back between Al's knees and looks upside down at him. When we go to Africa we *have* to visit Nairobi. It's very different now politically and in some ways socially since it became a member of the British Commonwealth.

Do tell, thought Al. The sweet whine in Julie's voice annoyed him at times. This was one. Who cares.

Barbara enters. She speaks generally to everyone then embraces her father. She kisses him. She then pecks a kiss on Deborah's cheek.

Deborah says, Did you have a good day?

We came in when the small craft warning went out.

Jim chuckles. He looks at Al. I hope you *didn't* learn anything about Julie you weren't supposed to know.

Would you like a jelly roll, Al.

No, Julie. Let's drive down to the Sound.

Great idea. I can show you that secluded part of the beach I told you about remember.

Who called while I was out? Barbara is half serious.

Here's the answer: Rea Dick Barry Vic Janice Ron Stella Hal Cindy Charles Gertrude. Wes Montgomery Clarence Snow Oscar Peterson Ann Gold Stan Getz Max Jones.

That's enough. Any messages. *I want a message.*

Julie tells her straight, The message is here always and it's always the same.

While deep sea diving I found a ship. It contained a sack full of pee weights hedge clippers a cupboard in the shape of a threshold a corner-whatnot shaped like an inlet a set of wrought-irons and forty-two beaded mirrors, wall size, plantation rockers with straw bottoms a stack of bright single-weave bedspreads a metal truck lined with rawhide a copper-dipper with a hole in it a painting of a white man by Julien Hudson a pine cigar-store Indian and a small wood carving of a woman pounding grain. I considered myself lucky.

"Personal space regardless of the paint on its surface," she said, "is an eyehole. A person is a picture of a mirror."

Patrick Blake is outside the drugstore at 2719 York Avenue nobody's on the street a hardness dullness coldness. Only the slightest warmth from a drugstore window where a woman's face flashes on and off. No teeth and a toothbrush moves back and forth across her nose the arm knocked two inches up out of place. Above the store shades to one room are down. I can't sleep I stand here looking to the other side at the railroad where the moon has turned the sky and the edges of the roofs green. Yellow and blue makes green so green I feel a chill. I walk into the station yard and look back at the drugstore. Patrick is still there in the fore-ground as the first light of morning falls down Main. Warm and still dark, his back finally against the red brick wall, he reads the prescription he has tried for thirty days to under-stand. It makes about as much sense as a lobster.

Roslyn is trying to take off her shoe. Jim is looking with

horror at his own face in the mirror one suspender hangs along his flat hip. In his right hand a toothbrush in the other a glass half filled with water.

They laughed at the doctor when he said he was a werewolf till he started barking at them. A delegation of women including Deborah approached him and asked him to do some dog tricks at their next meeting. He was delighted to tell them yes he would. He looked like Jim.

Again: a large seaside house red with red chimney shadows beneath window ledges under the roof of the porch along the sides under and behind the trimmings doors drain pipes.

Windows still damp from recent rain.

Soggy porch mosquitos drift along the floor. Deborah pushes a baby carriage along the flat hard cold boardwalk. Again and again: giant squatting doorways with pillows thick squatting windows with yellow shades white curtains line the way.

Roslyn passes before the red house the red house turns purple the ocean sends in a storm the wires running along the road snap. The window shutters everywhere shake the wires running along the road flap in the dust for a moment before everything is wet.

A little one-family white house at the top of the hill.

A church steeple floats in and rests on the beach.

The moon is a red broken car fender in the black sky. What else is new?

Cindy is in a juke joint. She is about to have a baby fall out of her. A fortune-telling woman wanders about inside the tavern. She predicts the baby will be a devil. It's coming out now. It's standing on the floor now alongside the drunk mother. The child is trying to open its eyes. It has its eyes open.

Jim is meeting with his secret connection from CIA headquarters in Virginia. They are whispering in the back room of a gift shop in downtown Darien. The connection says to Jim: It won't be Nick Zieff. It won't be Hourari. It will not be Barry Sands. Nor Janice Page. No way will it be Cindy. Nor Gail. The Black Professor is out of the picture. It won't be your brother-in-law Elmer. Nor your daughter's exlover Johnny Hawkins. Nor the drug pusher Allen Morris from Harlem. It won't be your son Oscar. Nor your favorite child Barbara. It won't even be Julie. The connection stops speaking and watches Jim. Jim is obviously puzzled. Then who will it be. The connection smiles his best secret smile.

I carried your mother across the threshold long before it was required by law, said Jim.

Oh dad you're so romantic. Are you really going to leave mom for that, that . . . other woman.

Julie, listen to me: there are things you don't understand.

. . . and Al chuckles and the phone rings and Jim rushes into the hallway—crossing the threshold—to answer.

Al watches Deborah's face. There is concrete transformation: the bricks melt into sawdust.

Deborah watches Al's hands. Hands that have fought rats, snatched purses from old ladies. Her eyes are jumpy and she is obviously straining to hear Jim's voice. She's on the couch sitting forward elbows on knees twisting her hands together as though trying to take off gloves.

Jim in the hallway is speaking softly. He cannot be heard in the family room.

When he finishes with the phone he says to Julie, would you like to come with me.

Where?

There's someone I want you to meet. He tries to smile.

Julie hesitated but finally got up from the floor and said, All right. By the way, I know where we're going.

Jim is displeased by her tone. His face shows his lack of pleasure.

On the way, in the Buick, Jim tries to explain *everything* to Julie: The place of the sacred doorway, its symbolism, why the ancient Jews needed secret codes and the "truth" concealed in some of these codes, especially information regarding the function of "Christ" and "Jesus" and the worship of fertility and the ultimate mystery of things and life.

He went on.' This situation we are involved in stems indirectly from certain Christian assumptions about the function and ritual of the in-and-out motion of things, negative and positive, life and death, rhythm and the static, the doorway and the door, the inlet and the exit, the turn-stile, the port and the land, the sea and the earth, the god and the virgin, the male and the female, being and not being.

Julie was awed by the wisdom of her father.

He went on. This situation we're in is being rendered in terms of images, and dramatic description. I am using very few things to represent other things. I think the meta-phor has its place but the place is historical. Yet I love the metaphor. I love its *visual* tendency. I want you, Julie, to understand that the ultimate *thingness* of our lives operates as a sort of *extended* metaphor.

She shook her head in agreement pretending to understand. Emotionally she understood intellectually she did not. She even said yes to make sure that he understood that she understood.

On he went. The Jewish people revolted against the Romans around A.D. 66 . . .

Julie looked out the window at a group of hunters going by on a path. Their rhythm kept them going on the curve of the path, over rock, through brush; deer and rabbit scattered out of sight. The dogs, their hawks, their spotted beasts ran faster than the beautiful horses they rode. These gallant hunters, dressed in silk and gold, moved into the forest, not with joy, but with a sense of duty. Grim faces. Birds broke from bushes and filled the sky with the blackness of their wings.

Barbara is in American History 301. The Black Professor is speaking to the class slowly but with a small amount of urgency: The thing to remember is that history is primarily fiction. Don't trust anybody who claims to know what happened. Nobody you know was there. And very likely, says the Black Professor, even those who were there did not know what was going on. Barbara looked out the school window. Black birds, about fifty of them, were crossing the sky.

Jim meets a stranger in a bar his name is Barry Sands this guy seems young idealistic Barry says no one hates the middle class more than the middle class and Jim thinks oh no another one who needs to listen to this young white Jewish dude still wet behind the ears but Barry goes on saying things like who hasn't gone back into the dirty clothes for a pair of clean socks

Barry Sands meets this older white-looking colored guy who has a nice smile Barry likes him but doesn't trust him in fact Barry doesn't trust people in bars period but he thinks this middle class colored man must have kissed a lot of ass to be where he's at and it's just so fucking disgusting to see this type of person who should be denouncing the system

Four tiny lakes are connected on the other side. Jim Ingram is the only one old enough to remember how it all happened. Next to the lighthouse is his house. By boat it is about twenty-five minutes. Linear in his outlook you can't talk to him about anything interesting.

The horn juts from the base of the house when it blows the grass waves in the yard the ocean turns yellow at its edges.

When you come from Connecticut you know about round windows with a crossbar or tiny square windows rectangles full of darkness as from closed eyes.

The sky is cloudy the horn never blows the gulls are restless they keep returning to scorched spots in the yard.

Jim is scared of his wife and daughters he sleeps in a shack out back surrounded by weeds and spiders.

Skinny and barefoot Patrick rubbed onions on his chest and was cured of lung infection. Strangers were his best friends.

This is a local experiment: ten people face a screen a picture is flashed before their eyes now the researcher asks what did you see. One lady sees a dog a man a boy riding a cactus plant a woman sees a man making girl scout cookies a young woman a young woman jumping from a diving board into a parking lot full of restless dogs a boy sees a woman pregnant in a doorway eating a watermelon men in doorways shooting dice it's Saturday men in doorways playing cards men in doorways holding children infants. Twin windows with twin girls in them giving men the eye. The researcher has locked his car stationed guards at the alley and in the hallway. The people don't trust the variables. The project looks funny the researcher Elmer Blake looks even funnier. His car is too clean and new who can trust him what is he after the boys the women the men the girls infants children. Who controls the control group. What's half of ten. What's half of five. What's half of two and one half. Is he trying to prove they don't know a hill of beans from a doorway.

Remember that boy in the red shirt. He lost respect for his parents and lost his job married Stella Della climbed the Hill but couldn't see the Plains. Took a bath in goose grease. Where one sheep leads the others follow. Joined the army and was killed on the front line.

love can take place in a place
that is not necessarily a hut
thanks to John K ashes and
dust and on the other hand it
is truly the triumph of imagination over smartness or is it
the smart set or love is a spell
of foolishness that doesn't
inspire laughter it is possible to
love even an animal this is not
an egg I mean exaggeration
even if a man has no reality
some woman might be there to
love him oh Ros don't you see
Deborah doesn't understand
me she said maybe we don't
truly understand each other
we have a mutual misunder-
standing temporary insanity
call it what you will and if we
are all alike what difference
does it make who we love or
who comes or comes into our
arms or what the dictionary
says about idyllic love or what
Freud says about its power to
lower self esteem or Raymond
Chandler's words about
throwing a Buick

I'm in a a glass phone booth in
Central Park you are riding
by on a bike and I see you
and call you screaming your
name but into the phone and
from here I realize I have a
womb with a view and it feels
safe and I continue to scream
your name hoping you'll hear
but I realize that for years and
years nobody's understood
me so I stop and start crying
knowing you too will not
respond or understand as you
wheel by on your ten-speed
looking so sheik and handsome and I'm so lonely and
crushed in the booth watching
you and trying to figure out
what you are thinking and
why I feel so shut out of your
life and why I'm in this booth
and you're riding along so
freely as though you didn't
have a care in the whole
world

If Jim and Al stand side by side they will almost certainly have a small shadow falling along the ground in front of them. Jim standing alone near a rock is likely to have more questions about the whole universe. Two trees on the horizon are so much more at peace.

The party is like this: Jim and Al stand talking with each other holding glasses containing liquor. The room is full of people who are not quite focused: one man's body suggests the need to be filled in with a pencil tracing the dots. A woman wears a lampshade for a hat. Al is uneasy with Jim. Jim is uneasy with Al. There is no fireplace with a robust fire to comfort them.

I have no special interest in Janice. I think she's a dodo. The bird. But one night out of boredom I call her. Out of control I say: If I walk fast in an easterly direction where will I end up? A place where the sky is full of fingerprints? Where pet cats climb the wall? Where everybody in town wears paper sacks over their heads with eyeholes for—you guessed it—eyes. No surprises here. I ask Janice if *three women* walk fast in an easterly direction what happens? She says they may *not* encounter an alligator eleven foot long. If someone speaks she says it doesn't mean that that person has a broad snout or is saying something. The caption above their heads where the words should ordinarily appear might be empty. Contact me for further explanation. I am always available.

"Sometimes, in truly brilliant fiction,

"The specific activities

"form is such a well-kept secret

"of the Central Intelligence Agency

"that it doesn't seem to exit . . ." —Z

"are a matter of some secrecy."
—Eugene J. McCarthy

Patrick and Oscar and other boys build a stairway for the owner of the steps fifteen of them work like hell. I am the owner.

Upstairs there are private windows that open into other rooms there are no doors nobody knows why.

You can't see the windows from the dean's office only the door downstairs and its never used boards are nailed across it.

The dean is talking on the phone to his wife she's at home eating candy from a heart shaped box how did he ever get himself into this mess the heat is so oppressive you'd think it is August.

Allen Morris's head is a private cave but he is unable to keep quietly inside: fat little women in g-strings and long black stockings keep leaping out of it in front of him onto the sidewalk dancing like crazy. His imagination has a borderline.

This house is hard and rough it is Jim's outer skin he is the heart beating in it he lights up inside. Warms his hands. The smoke burns his eyes.

Another light from outside falls along his chest his arms his ribs they are all planks. His arms like his ribs and his lungs still feel the vibrations of his children who grew up here, their naked feet pounding the floorboards. In and out across the threshold, outside the door on the porch a single towel hangs it holds the dirt of three generations and the love of four he no longer remembers not being here inside himself.

A living man disguised as a dead man dressed in the finest has no eyes as he strolls along unable to give in to the final death, if there is one. Death is a fresh onion.

You heard about the woman who died instantly upon looking in the mirror while wearing her wedding gown.

And the bride and the groom who saw each other before the ceremony. They were struck dead by lightning before the preacher could get to the church.

Elmer Blake wearing a Scottish cap black and white striped, puffs on a huge pipe. A lady follows him. A man in a derby follows her. Three strange men are walking fast toward the barbershop. Beer cans lace the gutter. Up high windows are left open. In one a man and a woman are fucking furiously.

The front door to the house is old, Blake's painted it red. There's a metal knocker in the shape of a child's hand. Above it a two-way peephole. Below it Gloria standing with back against lower panel. Gloria is withdrawn and frightened her eyes are large and dark. Inside the owner is singing . . .

Julie in a long white dress running across thick dark grass and children playing tag screaming. Three ladies sitting in a circle knitting. The old man slices the bread and pours the wine. Above, the clouds are scattered and moving fast. The smell of steak burning over coals.

Synthetic Blood, Inc. is the fastest growing blood business in town. The cost of goats lambs cows chickens dogs everything has gone up, up way up. Synthetic blood replaces real blood.

It's three in the morning buzzards circle over the funeral home. It's out of character. One lands on the threshold its beady eyes glowing in the moonlight.

The Threshold Print Shop and Art Gallery: Canvas thirty-two by twenty-four vase of chrysanthemums, shows influence of French Impressionist. In background a doorway with sunset. Canvas forty-eight by thirty: young woman bather. Shows influence of Renoir. Large soft pink breasts blue eyes heavy hips careless sky and sea meeting at the threshold of a blond wooded area.

Lying together in the small bed the house quiet Julie whispers to Al are you asleep.

No.

Across the hall in bed with his wife Deborah Jim was snoring. Once Barbara in her bed in her room blew her nose a loud honking.

Guess you know where I went with dad.

Roslyn's right.

Lying spoon fashion, for the one hundredth time Julie told Al the tortured story of Jim's romance with Roslyn and his plans to leave Deborah to marry Roslyn. Such exciting stuff. Al was gripped.

Julie stopped. She started again, on something else. You know, I wanted him to carry me across the threshold into her house but he refused. He never wants to *touch* me. I don't think he knows what touching is. I'm so glad you aren't like that. Touching is a very real part of our relationship.

She stopped and started again on Roslyn. Roslyn, she said, is using him and he can't see it he's a bigger fool than I thought he was. She's just a cheap white bitch that's all and he's losing his head over her she isn't worth it.

Al thought: Ah sleep it off.

She's been his secretary for something like ten years. He's really out of his mind. All those years he never thought of her that way now this. Coming back in the car I tried again for the one hundredth time to get him to see the light but he wouldn't let me talk said he didn't want to discuss it.

Al thought: Oh God.

I *did* tell Roslyn how I feel about the whole situation.

66

Woman to woman. Told her I thought she was very cruel to allow herself to wreck a beautiful marriage then she brought up this business about you and me and pointed out that you left Gail. I guess dad told her. Anyway she said she felt the same way about dad that I feel about you but it is *not* the same I told her it's simply not the same it's different!

Suddenly Al ran his finger into her.

Jim is a little boy his father is holding him up with both hands. "Look at the sun—no, I mean the moon," says Jim's father, "up there. See it, you see it. This is your lesson for today: that thing up there is definitely the moon. Got it? *Moooooon!*"

"The world is not an orderly place easily defined by a cozy myth," Jim tells Oscar who isn't listening. They're sitting on a log facing the lake. Oscar is playing with a stick. Bravely Jim continues: "If an alligator crawled toward the North Pole what would happen to its southeastern sense of things? Perhaps with luck the belly-crawling critter might reach eastern China where it would again feel at home. One cannot depend nor wait on luck. My father used to say this every Saturday morning. And I always turned to my mother for *her* bit of wisdom but she never offered it. She always said listen to your father."

From a telephone booth Al impulsively called Gail and said how are you. All right how are you what do you care anyway, Gail said. He said she said he said she said he said she said. She shouted into the phone: *You've ruined my life! You you*—And: I don't ever want to see you again. And still getting no response Gail said Allen can you hear me. Yes I hear you. And Gail whimpers, Allen I didn't mean it. I didn't really mean what I said. You can carry me across the threshold any day. I'll suck your toes. Cook your dinner. Hello soap opera. Hello toes dinner. Oh Allen I miss you so much oh God I'm so lonely. Allen is it true you're messing around with a white girl. Somebody told me that but I didn't want to believe it. I said oh no not Allen not Allen the revolutionary anybody but. Allen used his disgusted voice: No Gail, she's not a white girl. Is she a colored girl. Don't answer that if you don't want to. Sometimes I think I'm going out of my mind. Gail says, Ah to hell with this talk this is silly I shouldn't even be talking to you no way. Allen you don't care about me do you you care only about yourself I can't understand why you called it's silly foolish of me to talk with you like this but oh well I'm learning the hard way. Allen. He says, What. I, I don't know Allen are you all right where are you you don't want to tell me do you that's all right don't tell me it doesn't matter. Last night I dreamed you were killed it was a terrible nightmare. He said, Maybe you'd like to see it happen are you planning to keep the apartment. No Allen I'm not planning to stay here I can't stay here why are you coming back I mean when are you. He sighs. I might come back but I don't know when. Allen. Yes. I think you have another woman I know it. I think that's the reason you left me: another woman. Ruth told me this was going to happen. Ruth Ruth Ruth the ruiner. Fucking bigmouth stupidass bitch. Dumbass advice.

Outside the telephone booth a little white boy was wiggling a stick with a pink balloon attached to its end.

Gail believe me I wanted things to work out between us we were together two years that was two years of my life *too.* You think I was with you two years for nothing I really wanted things to work out and for two years baby I tried to get you to talk to me but you wouldn't say you couldn't you just wouldn't let me know what was on your mind. All you ever told me was what Ruth said and I didn't give a fuck about Ruth and at this point Gail . . . Gail says, Listen Allen if you called to argue you can just hang up I refuse to argue with you Allen why don't you stop kidding yourself stop trying to ease your guilt you know it was more than my friendship with Ruth you wanted me to be your slave and I refused that was the trouble and you wouldn't do your share and like a fool I supported you most of the time sure you had that little old jiveass poverty program job off and on but can't nobody depend on that kind of stuff I was just a fool is all I have to say a damn fool but I went along with you Allen cause I thought you meant well. Al says, Believe what you want to believe. Ah Allen stop trying to rationalize your own guilt. Gail, let me know when you move.

He almost cried.

Let me know *before* you move all right you can write to me at post office box number 780 Inlet, Connecticut. Allen, take care of yourself all right. I will. You take care of *yourself.* I worry about you, Allen. Worry about yourself. Sometimes I think I might go out of my mind but the truth is even at the worse times I somehow know deep down that I'll be all right I'll survive all this.

That's good to hear.

Take care.

I will. Bye.

Goodbye Allen.

Jim is feeling very tense feels he needs a drink he stops in a bar. Humphrey Bogart is there leaning against the bar. Bogart tries to smile at Jim but his face doesn't quite make it. Bogart lifts his glass to Jim once Jim has a drink in his hand too. Bogart says, "I don't trust bastards who don't drink." Jim says, "I'll drink to that. By the way what's your name?" Before Bogart can answer this perfectly logical question Roslyn rushes into the tavern. She looks frantic but also a little like Lauren Bacall in one of the early movies. Roslyn, not as Bacall would do, grabs Jim's arm and says, "The car's waiting outside—we'd better go, *fast!*" As they leave Bogart waves and shouts, "*Happy sailing!*"

After Tony swept the butcher shop he went home to his wife and ten children. Small beady eyes and a thick nose. They looked like him. The sun follows him everywhere he goes. He has lumps at the rear of his skull. The sun loves to follow him. The Ingrams like to buy their meat at his shop.

Alla Blake carries a dagger dripping blood and people say a woman she's not strong enough to have done it somebody put the knife in her hand look at her she's frail. Her robust husband Elmer keeps a rosewood stick alongside his plate at the dinner table. He's carving faces into it every minute he has the chance. I told you all this before.

The Black Professor with scales rather than skin slits open the belly of a giant fish and a pack of tiny brown and yellow people slide out like sardines, a mob of naked women rush them with giant bunches of grapes prying open their mouths forcing them to eat.

Piles of rotten fruit lie wasted along the edge of the river while overhead dragons float complete with seats and seatbelts and passengers secure with credit cards. This is not one of Oscar Ingram's weird dreams.

This thing that moves beneath the surface changes color— once when it got stuck between two rocks the water all around it turned red, a fantastic red like red you have never seen. It amazes me.

That man who spent so much time playing with the shell got caught in it and cried for days but nobody believed he was serious till they smelled his remains and cracked open the shell. He looked just like Jim.

"If we go on living among the blind we too will forget how to see," Deborah says, "nobody will ever see us again."

Elves and goblins dance around the legs of Jim and Roslyn who are getting high on the holy plant the amanita muscaria having visions talking to themselves.

A pig-like creature runs about trying to dislodge a bird-like thing clinging to its back. There's nothing I can do to help it.

Official things: across the threshold of every city office steps a serious person. The mayor of the city planner the city editor the city clerk the people of the city room of the city newspaper.

Unable to follow her mother Julie follows in her father's footsteps, they lead into the softest, most beautiful women she's ever seen.

Something scratches at the back door of Julie's memory trying to get in.

Still inside: it's Inlet County and warm armpits. *Swing your mate!* Walls sweat the wallflowers hug them rub them scrape them and claw them. Polished hard floor shakes beneath the hillbilly band. Lonely girls cling to secrets of breeding held firmly in the backs of their heads by the stillness of their tongues. They fox-trot thrust and strut and make circles, boys bob and twitch lips fingers toes, holding back a solid wall of faces blushing or closing, closing and opening. Minds full of pink bloomers and white pumps ruffles and ribbons. Roslyn watches from a bench. She's sad.

At the center of the carnival is a large uncracked egg, inside we hear music.

A furious large plant crawls along the earth trying to follow the warmth of the sunlight. Barbara, watching it, tries to do the same.

The people down in the control room keep asking if there is an upward swing, a sort of tension that builds. People who have been away for days thinking about this have no answer. I have.

"Door. A feminine symbol which, notwithstanding, contains all the implications of the symbolic hole, since it is the door which gives access to the hole; its significance is therefore the antithesis of the wall. There is the same relationship between the temple-door and the altar as between the circumference and the centre: even though in each case the two component elements are the farthest apart, they are nonetheless, in a way, the closest since the one determines and reflects the other. This is well illustrated in the architectural ornamentation of cathedrals, where the facade is nearly always treated as if it were an altar-piece."

—J. E. Cirlot,
A Dictionary of Symbols

"Threshold. A symbol of transition and transcendence. In architectural symbolism, the threshold is always given a special significance by the elaboration and enrichment of its structure by means of porches, perrons, porticoes, triumphal arches, battlements, etc., or by symbolic ornamentation of the kind which, in the West, finds its finest expression in the Christian cathedral with its sculpted mullions, jambs, archivolts, lintels and tympana. Hence the function of the threshold is clearly to symbolize both the reconciliation and the separation of the two worlds of the profane and the sacred. In the East, the function of protecting and warning is effected by the 'keepers of the threshold'—dragons and effigies of gods or spirits. The Roman god Janus also denoted this dualism characteristic of the threshold, which can be related analogically to all other forms of duality. Hence the tendency to speak of the threshold between waking and sleeping."

—Ditto

"Door signs / Objects may be placed over or above a door according to the community's lore. The horseshoe appears in various parts of America and tramps have been suspected of leaving signs that indicate to their fellows where to expect good meals or where to avoid harm from dog or man."

—Marjorie Tallman,
Dictionary of American Folklore

"Door of the dead. A portal built in a house for the express purpose of removing a dead body from the dwelling in order that the ghost will not be able to find its way back to haunt the survivors. This door is ordinarily sealed up again after the corpse has been taken out."

—Charles Winick,
Anthropology

Door closers and checks—repairing.
Door frames.
Door operating devices.
Automatic Doorways.
Entrance Controls, Inc.
Entry Systems.

—Seattle, Washington
*Pacific Northwest Bell
Telephone Book,* 1976

"1. Architrave
2. Top rail
3. Shutting stile
4. Hanging stile
5. Top panel
6. Frieze rail
7. Muntin
8. Middle panel
9. Lock rail
10. Bottom panel
11. Bottom rail

Fig. 39 Door"

—John Fleming, Hugh Honour,
Nikolaus Pevsner,
—*The Penguin Dictionary of Architecture*

"I have opened the door for many colored people."

—Jim Ingram

"I know thy works: behold, I have set before thee an open door, and no man can shut it: for thou hast a little strength, and hast kept my word, and hast not denied my name."

—*Revelations* 3:8

1. I probably won't say any of this again. I want to try to explain to you how I feel about myself.

2. Try to be patient with me. I know I don't always make sense.

3. I feel that I have to know and feel more than I feel. I keep trying to understand my feelings.

4. Going to work depresses me. I hate it.

5. Even at night when you're asleep I'm awake crying and I can't stop. I feel all bottled up like I'm choking to death.

6. I have to bother you with all of this because I know you can't help me. I used to think that if we made love more that might help.

7. My depression frightens me. I can't understand it.

8. I don't like for you to introduce me as your wife. That bothers me too. I'm not your wife.

9. My self image is at stake. My sense of myself. My feelings. What I feel. How I feel what I feel.

10. I'm not trying to make you feel guilty. You are not to blame.

11. I want a vision of myself that I can live with. I am a person. A *real* person. I have to somehow learn to *believe*

that then maybe things will change.

12. Does this make any sense?

13. There are certain incidents in my mother's past that she will not talk about. That depresses me, too.

14. My father drinks too much. All my friends have fathers who drink too much.

15. When I was a child I played alone. I'm still alone.

16. Our sex life is not all it should be. We could try harder. *You* could do better. Jim are you listening?

17. I want to get married. I'm getting older. I need the security. I want to marry you and spend the rest of my life with you.

The trucks are filled with women who have violated the threshold law they are being transported to the woods to serve time maybe a week, ten days certainly not more. Blue trucks yellow trucks white trucks. All day they leave the city for the country. None of the women are crying. Some shake their fists at the photographers.

As the mayor is making his speech on the threshold law a hugh monster breaks into the television studio and rips the mike from his hands. It says, *We're celebrating what we don't know*—that's what it's about! The mayor's face is tight with laughter that feels like fear.

At the Night Club castrati sing sweet country songs in Italian. A man who coughed broke a long slit in their voices they had to whisper for weeks till a used car salesman repaired them.

At the Open Door people on stage are the same as those in the audience. It's confusing because each would like to know the difference between the subject and the background.

But it does not matter since everybody goes to the Renaissance or the Rib Joint where you can get anything and give anything you want to give.

A brisk wind was moving the bright green grass a few clouds hung low the road in the distance was yellow orange, an old car was moving along it. Jim, Oscar and Patrick on beautiful black horses were moving along at a canter, Jim fell into a trot, watching the car on the road. They came to the threshold of a drawbridge and the horses got nervous they refused to cross. Jim beat his horse brutally. Streaks of blood shone on the animal's hindside as it threw him into the road and kicking up a cloud of dust, took off across the bridge alone. The other two riders and the other two horses were stunned as they watched.

My wife likes grapes. You don't say. Yup. How about your wife? Lost her legs and arms during the war have to feed her use my fingers mash up the cornbread in the greens. You don't say.

The frontier is the threshold to my body. Pushing, I push the trees away, plow the land drive the tribes out drive out all the animals, the wilderness is mine. I command the frontier. Here at the edge of settled regions there is a feeling, something is about to happen. As a frontiersman I learn how to change the pain the mystery you wouldn't believe. What's out there. Is it in here. What is this pulling sensation. Why do I wake up at four every morning searching for my title to the land.

Barry Sands talks about pubic hair all the time. Claims to know more about it than anybody large prints of it decorate his living room. A single man with no children he has never lifted a woman across the threshold. He listens to threshold music on the radio and eats scrambled beef and listens to a large silver clock ticking in the back.

You remember how Roslyn was drying her feet well she's still at it. The light changes but the room is still pastel, yellow and green and blue and warm pink. From the threshold outside through the keyhole a peeping tom is watching her delicate movements, her arm, her feet. She smells of mint. When she sees the eye in the keyhole she smiles gently.

Cynthia Neal picks up her purse and leaves her house by way of the front door. Her lover José Cruz comes from the side of the house and follows her—careful to stay out of her sight. A voice in his head is telling him to do this weird thing. The voice sounds like Julie's voice. It says: she is betraying you she is headed for a secret meeting with a man named Barry Sandstone. They will become lovers. Be careful you are about to lose her. Here's a knife stab her in the back. José looks around for the knife but of course there is no knife. Meanwhile Cynthia enters a supermarket to do her shopping. The African is there puzzling over what to buy. Jose turns back deciding that he has lost his marbles. Maybe it was that umbrella he borrowed that has caused this silliness.

THE ANNUAL DOOR AND THRESHOLD CONFERENCE
of Inlet Characters on
The Problems of Emergencies

Monday and Tuesday
December 31 &
January 1, 19—

SCHEDULE

Monday, December 31

9:45   Orientation

10:00   Opening Address—The Author's Persona

10:30   The Way Things Are: An Overview

       Roslyn Carter: Mr. Ibsen: How To Play
       James Ingram: Mr. Hamlet: How To Be Played
       Julie Ingram: Mr. Cervantes: How To Be First

11:45   Who Decides Which Thresholds Get Crossed?

       Barry Sands: Stephen B. Courage: Imagine War
       Patrick Blake: Wolf Larsen: Imagine The Sea
       Barbara Ingram: Louis Treasure: Friday Or
       Saturday Or Sunday?

1:00   Lunch

2:15   Can Serious Characters And The Casual Author
       Co-Exist?

       James Ingram: Nobody Knows My Character
       Guest Speaker: Harriet Cabin: Old Colored Men I
       Have Known

3:00   Does An Inlet Citizen Need To Be Represented?

       Julie Ingram: Views Of My Father Sleeping
       The Black Professor: Booker T.: Nothing Beats A
       Good Story

Joe and Sadie: Brenda Starr: I Represent Myself—
You Can Too!

4:00　How Are Emergencies Really Handled?

Barry Sands: A Tribal Jew: On Removing The Bell
Allen Morris: Manchild In Connecticut
Janice Page: Mosquitos Are Not The Worst

January 1

10:00　Who Decides Which Doors Get Opened and What
Happens When They Get Open?

Deborah Ingram: The Best Years Of Our Lives
Guest Speaker:　Rudy Nog: Barking Up The *Right*
Tree And What It Gets You
Guest Speaker: O. Motorman: Threshold Music
May Be Bad For Your Health

11:30　Who Stands Up For The Small Emergencies In Life?

The Black Professor: How Not To Be Like A
Hemingway Character
Gloria Blake: Gertrude Douglas: All The Big
Moments
Barry Sands: How To Get Out Of The Circus

1:00　Lunch

2:00　Who Decides Which Symbols Of The Doorway Get
Used?

Deborah Ingram: New Gateways And The Women's
Movement
The Black Professor: Hard Work and Clean Living

Barbara: I Have A Dream (Dream Me!)

3:00   To What Extent Should Inlet, Connecticut Hold
        Itself Responsible For Its Condition? An Unnamed
        Character: What Is Its Condition?

        Guest Speaker: Van Gogh In Inlet: Lust For Form
        Alla Blake: Smitty: Call Me Ishtar: Mother Of Us All
        The African: Frankie: Sin and Stones May Break
        My Bones But Doors Will Never Hurt Me

4:00   Who Decides Where It All Begins And Ends?

        Nicholas Zieff: King K.: Power and Powerlessness:
        The Plight Of The Ugly Lover Of Inlet
        Rea: An Echo From The Past: Hot Breath
        Vic: Our Origins: The Lusty Centaur
        James Ingram: Professor Charles: Our Origins:
        The Green Algae

        Conclusion: To Be Announced.

I WILL ATTEND THE CONFERENCE

Name _____

Dates _____

Organization _____

Address _____

City _____ State _____ Zip _____

Night life in Inlet is for the birds topless joints and that's it
what else can I tell you chicks hang out in doorways. Then
when you are not looking for that, when you're not vulgar,
the museum is closed. They lock the doors and throw
parties for bigshots.

Men with their hair cut short fall drunk in chairs without
bottoms. This happens a lot at Ned's Eatery. Ned is dead
his son makes hamburgers and frenchfries and malts with a
knife lying alongside the cashbox.

The Salvation Army woman keeps singing all these silly
songs in my ear then retreating to the safety of her wind-
swept doorway.

"Flashes of people—not even *real* people," he said,
"responding to a complex situation where a certain motif is
persistent . . ."

I went under the bridge Jim walked across it. This *can* go on.

Following the prayer there was a news show. The screen
closed out everything else happening in the world.

I wash my clothes and water the plants. The Holy Ghost
lives next door. Down the hall the Threshold Law writer
has a secret apartment where he brings his mistresses. He's
married to a fat woman way across town who is good to
him. She reads him the Letters of Paul. They open doors in
his head. But the Good Samaritan opens *her* eyes!

The word spreads. In Darien and Bridgeport in Canaan Woodbury Stamford Monroe Fairfield the word spreads fast: the trains are late: in Silver Spring there are no trains. There are shopping centers full of places with glass doors you can see through glass doors. The Circumcision of The Gentiles took place yesterday in the doorway of a shop in the shopping center across the street. The Whore of Babylon slept next door. The trumpets of doom are heard constantly down the hall. Doors closed or not.

The killer slept in the sauna waiting for Deborah to arrive. Roaches crawled into his mouth.

The Ingram family is exploring the mountains nearby. Camping equipment attached to their backs. Clouds move swiftly overhead.

During the summer I see from the streets of Inlet people in windows looking down on other people. Boys sitting in doorways. In one window only the tip of a face. An elbow. An arm. A leg. A small portion of somebody's back.

Small raggedy Indian children are chasing Barry Sands on the beach. They're barefoot it's fun. Barry drunk stumbles and falls and rolls in the sand laughing. The kids climb on his chest and walk up and down. They can't stop giggling they stuff shells and pebbles into his mouth. Seaweeds sprout from his ears.

Julie is speeding along an isolated country road in a light blue Dodge, current model. Pavement hot grey. I'm watching her. Trees grass bushes a thick dark green splash of earth on the far side. She is going upstate to . . . at the gas station she stops, asks the attendant, how do you . . .

Robot Repair Shops, Inc., have sprung up all over Inlet. A chain of them owned by two brothers who live in Florida. Business is fantastic robots break down more often than cars.

As though driven by a state of madness Barry is making a list of words starting with the letter Z: Zombie Zlokobinca Zen Zener Zendavesta Zozo Zlito Zabulon Zapan Zardust Zlata Zeus Zohar Zollner Zoether Zodiac Zugen Zwaan Zuccarini Zola and Zekerboni. He yawns as he loses interest in the Z's. He falls asleep there on his couch. Julie appears in his sleep. She speaks: Through the Z you have connected to the underworld of the snake. And since I am a creature of the water and the sky you have greatly reduced your chances of possessing me. Too bad for you sucker!

Jim Ingram was again dreaming. He was back in Africa in his office there. Ten years of respect, sane and clean. People appreciated his power. He appreciated his own power. Power is as hard as rock. He could smell his own rot, too. Even before he was thirty. In the dream his age doesn't matter. He was busy designing the Black American Dream. Three hundred and twenty-seven versions of it lined up in his sleep every night. The shadow of Martin Luther King loomed over them and over Jim. In the back seat of each dream Deborah was always making love to a snapshot of Booker T. Washington.

Even in his dream Jim was an expert at collecting information for the United States. In this particular dream he is about to have a run-in with the natives.

To distract himself he builds model slaveships with matchsticks and glue. His three year old daughter Julie watches his pink fingers. His wife is pregnant with a child they plan to call Barbara or Oscar. Names of grandparents.

He waters the plants.

The threshold to his home has been blessed by the bishop. It has been blessed again by Martin.

A naked girl small and lovely is lying in the bed of his mind. A raven is pecking at her eyes. He feels castrated as he watches. Someone in the back is playing Mozart on the piano. His pregnant wife has a loose vagina. He sleeps with his back to her. He snores.

Here in this scene out of guilt he takes Deborah to Nick Tamucci's for dinner. The waiters sing happy birthday. Deborah cries she is so happy.

He is a matchstick agent who has measured his life out with peanut butter spoons. His African secretary chews beechnut chewing gum. When he listens to her scratch her leg he feels like crawling out of his skin. He sends her out for coffee. She comes back with tea.

The dream locks him in these years of diapers and baby shit. And the sound of crying off and on all night. The natives are getting closer.

Deborah is talking to him as he sleeps: "I am locked in prison eating ham and spinach and I write crude letters to you outside. I fear constipation fatigue psychosis withdrawal brain damage delusions and panic. Can you help me."

Jim continues to snore. The natives are too close for comfort.

He is possessed by the machinery of his dream. There is a boy in his head cutting the strips of the dream with an automatic blade. The strips are like white flesh without blood. Dust settles on his eyelids. The buzz saw cuts right through the dream and Jim is in terror.

Jim's fingers are relatively short and nervous and they sweat. His thin hair grows thinner. He dreams of balding. In these dreams the natives cause all the problems he's having with his hair and the sweat. They use magic on him. Don't they realize he's fighting for their rights too.

I give Jim all the rope he needs.

He rests his head on the top of his desk. There is a view of his wife weeping. She's sitting up in bed weeping. She's holding her big belly. And weeping.

The black office boy comes and says to Jim: "The cigars old men smoke are going to be taken from them one of these days then the whole world will reach its turning point, the threshold will revolve."

Jim smirks. "Shine my shoes."

The natives are now outside his office. He can *feel* them. He can smell their sweat. They are about to break down his door and fill his office with their blackness. He can already see them going through his files attempting to understand the scribblings and typewritten marks on the many sheets of paper in the folders. In one version of this dream he is so scared he is about to pee on himself. In another he welcomes them, passing out cigars and slapping them on their backs.

Deborah says, "My dress is so soaked in blood it sticks to my body. How did this happen to me why me."

Jim tells her, "Go home. This is no place for a lady."

The natives beat at his door.

He hides all his versions of the Black American Dream in the closet. At this point the door falls into the room.

Deborah shakes him and he comes out of it running for his life. It's always this way.

"My mouth tastes like I've been drinking horse piss or something," he says.

"That's my line." Deborah smiled. "I have to say that I do more than live with deflated breasts or that I hold my orgasm away from my body." She held him to her breasts. "Tell me your nightmare."

"They led me into the fire."

"Were Egyptians building pyramids in the distance?"

"Yes. And the natives were unhappy again. As they beat at my door the breather called on the telephone again just breathing and not saying anything."

"Did all this happen before you worked for Pussy Superior or—"

"Superior Pussy."

"I mean. Did it happen before."

"No it was after the threshold company when I was in college. The dream takes place in Africa. My guilt. My white skin. No African believes me when I say I'm black. I want to cry."

She hugs him. "You're a *human being* honey don't worry about them. Play with your matchsticks. I love you."

"I love you too."

Under the covers they touched toes.

Jim sends Roslyn Carter (in his place) to address a group of businessmen on the problems of Information Service. In the middle of her talk she blushes because she feels her period starting and she is unprepared. The men notice the change in her color and some of them think she's sweet to be so shy.

Roslyn is on the bus going back to the office. She's returning from the hairdresser's. She's writing in her diary: "The weather is fair, what is unfair is the climate: the ride is safe and sunny, but I'm blue. This town should make me happy but it doesn't. A girl's hair dries fast in the light. There are white sales and there is Jim. I grew up in Boulder where gangs of deer stand at the edge of the road watching Dodge cars and Ford pickups. The Mountains are sturdy. But I don't miss any of it."

Near a stone doorway I gain strength. Obviously in the back woods: two women stand at a gate feeding pigs. The pigs grunt and grind their thick ears of corn. I stand behind Jim Ingram watching his brush strokes. His impression is not the same as mine.

A floating gin palace is moving slowly through the sky over our house. On its bow these large red letters: The Nickel-Plated Threshold With Nothing Lost To Honor. People on shore wave and catcalls and whistles are returned by deck-hands and mopboys eyes peep from portholes.

In Inlet, Connecticut we are eating bread and listening to passionate gypsy music the skyline is met by a strip of hot yellow sand the beach, our mouths, openings, are receiving our crumbs.

A thug with a hat pulled down over his eyes goes into a restaurant where the walls are filled with signs saying pie chocolate beans beef bouillon hamburger enjoy yourself the cook is in the kitchen way back there you can't see him the doors are closed. The thug takes a seat the waitress picks up a tip and drops it into her pocket, a dark warm hole. The pocket closes around her hand.

Inside the jukebox a singer is singing when money is inserted he swallows it. The shift changes every eight hours.

I grunt and laugh the girls in the sand box next to me giggle and punch each other playfully then we exchange sand boxes. I am deep in their sand box and feel the heat left by their bodies.

The church-feeling is strong now that the church has fallen. It fell. One woman lost her drawers later found them and split the doors are locked and people can't get in like in the old days when everybody trusted everybody.

My mother stands in the doorway of the toystore. I had to return the things I stole.

A giant threshold may one day be erected over our lives.

Messengers, on horseback, ride through the cold night, death and leather held in a firm embrace. Each section of the dream shifts turns. The disruption comes at the moment when nothing can hold back the blood chilled flowing down out of the body as the eyes close, heavy. And unless the body is held in a great embrace everything— really everything—goes down.

The ulcer has a face and a personality. It is a hole pulsing deep in the brain where light is a switchblade knife cutting through a silk shirt on Saturday night. I watch Allen Morris the nervous witness.

Jim checks his watch. Face hard as red paint or cold lipstick. Dick Tracy nose. What is it time for?

Deborah noticed blood in her urine. *How many times?* Do you feel any pain.

Jim stood at the door light fell. I believe in . . . He went inside and locked the door. They heckled him, threw rocks and bottles. *I have no sacraments: I have no creeds . . .*

Card tables are erected between people over fifty. There are poker games and whiz and checkers. Dim lights are turned on the domes of their heads and the surface of the tables. Hands rest, holding stiff cards. Eyes often are heavy and droopy. Some actually fall asleep. Mostly though eyes measure eyes. Ears lift at the sound of meaningful coughs.

Deborah is desperately lonely in the house pacing the floor. If only the African were here. Jim is a lost cause. I pity him. No I don't pity him. I need to be fucked. I'm lonely. I need to be loved. A face appears at the window. She screams. She runs from the room. She locks the front door then hides in the basement. For two hours. When she returns to the living room the face is still there. It's Jim's.

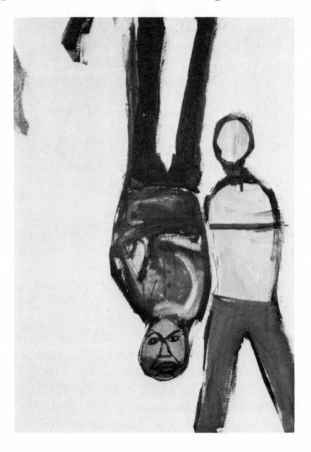

Al received in the mail an envelope containing a scrap of dirty paper torn from the edge of a brown bag. On it was scribbled: *Allen I've split. You better come and see about your apartment or what ever you plan to do. Gail.*

Al received an envelope containing a picture of two young women photographed while pissing on a diamond-studded threshold in City Hall. The arresting officer said they did not resist arrest.

Deborah, who was at Duck Pond for the weekend, drove Al to the bus station where he caught the early bus for New York.

The bus was full of confederate soldiers, misplaced in time, headed for the Civil War. Al was puzzled out of his mind. He asked one what's going on. The guy laughed and said they were in a play called *Stonewall.* Another one started explaining how Mussolini's soldiers cut a doorway through *The Last Supper.* That too, he said, was a stonewall.

They got off at Walt Disney Way.

Al relaxed he thought of Deborah she was elegant. Really respect her spirit. He looked out the window trying to see the landscape but saw Deborah. Ah come on now Al she's your girl's mother almost an old woman old enough to be your mama. Hello Deborah. What a name. He closed his eyes and there she was there too. Clearer. So he stopped fighting her and let her stay there. Welcome to the madness. Meanwhile the bus hit the turnpike and he opened his eyes: farmhouses redbarns cows in clusters grazing in open fields, display signs suddenly jutting out from the roadside. Now rocky hillsides or a sudden grove of sweetbirch and blackbirch.

He got off at the edge of midtown. At the bus stop a

hotel called The Other Side, over its doorway, announced: *All Night Visitors Welcome. In business since 1969.*

His apartment was strange. No one was there. He looked in the closets expecting King Kong or the Green Hornet and discovered that not only had Gail taken all of her own clothes and things she had taken half of his. Why. The rug the TV the dishes the knives forks glasses tea cups even the plants, everything gone. This was an airless place. There was no soap not even a towel in the bathroom. She'd left the light on in the bathroom. He turned it off and went to turn on the radio but it too was gone. He wanted to cry. Just as he was about to leave the blast of the telephone shocked him. At the same moment he noticed on the floor beside the couch a used crusty prophylactic. He felt like a character in adult fiction all the pain jealousy rage, the whole bit.

It was Gail. So what do you do call here all day every day how did you know. I didn't she said I just had an impulse to call so I did I don't know why how are you Allen and when did you get back.

As she talks small-talk he tries to *see* her. There she is in a tight Macy's skirt her wide hips long black legs, he sees one side of her beautiful face smooth face. She's saying something about the silliness of game playing and he says Hey let's drop this we never get anywhere. With the toe of his shoe he pushes the prophylactic out of sight. He changes the subject. Where are you at work. No I didn't go in today I'm staying in the apartment in the . . . never mind. I'm staying with a friend. I got scared of being alone. Scared of myself especially at night.

Liar.

How's Booker he says, fine she says, he's sitting right here looking up into my face you know how he does that such a pleading, dependent look.

Al sees the dog, the evil bitch. He looks at the scar on the back of his right hand where the animal's teeth once caused blood to flow.

The dull conversation drags on till Gail says Allen I'm going to hang up now take care okay. I will. You too. And I love you. Don't say that Allen please let me try to get over you. And now Booker is barking and Gail explains. Somebody's at the door goodbye Allen. Bye I'll be in touch.

He thought of calling his mother on her job at the hospital but changed his mind to hell with it. I need a joint. The phone rang again. Hello is Grandma Moses there.

No this is Normal Rockwell speaking can I help you.

He still wanted to cry like he'd seen his father cry years ago. There was his father sitting there on the side of the bed crying saying that the mental institution was worse than all the jails and prisons. That desperate feeling of helplessness he felt then was on him again.

The phone rang again and he walked out without answering it. He closed his eyes in response to the afternoon sunlight hugging the edge of a building. He walked to the corner and stood there unable to move, to cross the street. Cars kept shooting by heading north. One way. This is *me* I don't know what I'm doing but I got to keep doing it. He thought of Julie and the tears came.

He was gloomy when Julie picked him up in her mother's white four-door Chevy. She was sensitive to his mood and on the way back didn't question him. When they reached Duck Pond Al made a very deliberate effort to be friendly. They got out and went in. Barbara was here now so was Deborah.

That night the four of them went to a rock concert. Janis Joplin was the star. When Janis came out she started into her thing right away her hair wild and dressed in gaudy clothes. With the microphone in her right hand her act transformed the listeners from supportive audience to frenzied mob. The audience was ninety-nine percent white. Al felt out of place. Deborah kept trying to reassure him that it was all new to her, too. Julie and Barbara were old hands at this and in their excitement hardly noticed Al's and Deborah's bewilderment.

Janis ended the show by burning a hugh gold threshold on stage and then throwing the hot ashes down into the audience. Thousands of kids screamed trying to eat the stuff.

it's all been done before nothing new Sterne Melville Kafka even earlier I tell my characters but they're not interested they're interested in each other Jim for example right now is depressed thinks he's a hard red crab bleeding in the sun an insane man sitting beneath a table crying he's in bad shape

I suspect, Ros, that the narrator of this book spends his free time watching slit fish in window sunlight and he crushes snails and seashells and buys straw baskets and blue china fine as it comes and gold bowls meant to stay empty and I think also that this guy isn't really interested in us but in those sorts of things things he can touch wet and dry things beautiful objects

The fat people are here the Inlet Con-Game Steak House Restaurant and the County Tavern and Nick Tamucci's and, wouldn't you know, here's Andrew Grippo, who weighs four hundred pounds. It's not enough that they are here they are involved in the secret reorganization of . . . you know what.

Out on the river a slaveship goes by. On it there are thousands of small chairs made by slaves for dolls.

It's raining the street lamps have been broken by hoodlums a bunch of kids are jumping rope and playing hide and seek.

Jim was an old man who sat alone near the doorway of his house in his back yard and he had gone eighty-four days without moving. Children on the road whisper lady next door whispers say he's crazy they feel sorry for his wife.

After everything has fallen to pieces Jim stands against the door hoping for something different something new to happen. Deborah throws knives into the door against which he stands the knives form an outline of his body just missing him each time.

He was an old man who stood alone against a door full of knives and knife marks. The dagger thrower stops for lunch goes down to The Conflict and Control Snackbar for a hamburger and a Coca-Cola.

Jim's wife the children the lady next door went to Jim in

silence seeing him unharmed they decided there was no reason to put him back together again. When all the king's men arrived they were sent home.

Roslyn Carter thinks she has all the answers she speaks with authority: "Your lifelong family dentist knows less about your mouth than the person who kisses you once in the dark the person who knows you is the one who wipes your ass."

The nightwatchman is lonely.

Roslyn sat alone at a cafe table smoking a cigarette. The smoke went deep into her lungs, it lingered there touching the walls.

Rows of dry skull bones bleached in the sun. Along the walkway the researchers have made a fence of them.

Roslyn with blond hair crosses a grey plaza. She feels her mink watching every man who leaves or enters. She can weigh which ones are worth following. "In another sense none of them are."

The man who watches her during the day is also lonely.

Her dress was so soaked in his blood it stuck to her body, she left the hatchet alongside the body.

Roslyn with blond hair crosses a grey plaza. She feels naked. A dog sleeps near the fountain. It continues to sleep. In this strange street she has no idea where she is going.

Harry Weiss better known as Harry Houdini magically appears one night in Roslyn's bedroom. Roslyn is sitting up against two pillows reading *Against our Will,* a very thick book. Houdini says I'm Harry and I've come to help you. Mercy me says Roslyn I sure need it. Exactly what do you need. How many wishes do I have. I'm not that kind of magician lady. I can do amazing feats of escape. I can even help you escape from the mess you're presently in with this fella called Jim. What'd you say you want out of this situation—do you want a new life. Roslyn shows him her serious face. Certainly. Okay this is what you do: you must go out and gather together a wide variety of herbs here are the names write them down sage forest manna rue orris root lungwort suntull enzian malaxis meadow mint alsine christianwort and wormwood. Make a tea of all of these at the same time and drink it and in twenty-four hours you will be liberated from this indecisive bastard secret agent! And at this point Harry disappears just as suddenly as he had appeared.

Now while Julie was down flat on her stomach on the raft on the water under the bright sun basking naked, oblivious to the world, Al sat moody sprawled in a chair on the deck of the little house, idle. Through the trees he could see Julie. Bitch. I love her. I love the bitch. Some day she will drive me nuts. The smell of the damp earth from a recent rain filled the air.

How do you know any of this is true—does it matter? It is all true and it matters.

Julie's hair and shoulders are true. Al sees them. Hi there shoulders! Then her legs and feet. But her hair, what lovely hair! Silky long brown hair soft and straight. She tried a bush and she tried an afro but the texture was too soft. It wouldn't keep. Wants to prove she's Black. It's all right baby, I know. Maybe you don't but the whole world knows. Only the shadow knows. Who knows the troubles I've seen.

Al hadn't gone down to bask in the sunlight with Julie because he figured he was dark enough. Ten years ago: the kids on the playground kidding him about being so black. Growing up in Harlem is a bitch. Now he was mentally Black but was he truly proud of it of Africa. They still showed the white king of the jungle on television. And when razor toting niggers get drunk they still call each other low down black motherfuckers. Al felt out of it. He looked out beyond Julie to the other side of the lake. Clouds were forming.

How do you know any of this . . .

He looked at Julie. She was now reading. Intense reading was something he'd never developed any interest in. Julie and her Jane Austen Joseph Conrad Charles

Dickens Thomas Hardy and Virginia Woolf. I can't get interested in that shit. What is this restlessness, this churning . . . inside; where does it come from. I should have a car then I could drive and drive and drive, drive it out. Get some good smoke and drive.

He went inside for no particular reason. There was Julie's diary. Why not. She wouldn't mind. She *asked* me to read it. With it, Al went out on the deck. Maybe I'll find a clue to Miss J. Miss J the Mystery Lady. Colored but not like any colored person I've known. Heard about them. Saw them at a distance. What'd she see in me.

How do you know . . .

Julie's neat handwriting:

I wish dad would for once reveal himself to me. I think, if he could do that, I could love him well. I dreamed last night that he made love to me behind some bushes. Why. Al looked up at the trees, stunned.

. . . It is all true.

When the doorbell rang I hid the shotgun. Through the window I saw them still playing golf at the Municipal Golf Course.

Their heads were covered to protect them from the desert sun. They crossed the threshold into the city.

The dog warden signed his name on the dog paper and gave it to Janice she brought it to me then closed the door. Bits of light and color cling to the emptiness. I went out and got in the car. The dog looked at me and barked. I barked back.

Hummmmmmmm, smells good, Deborah said. Whatya cooking. I saw Jim running toward the house. On the other side the road was empty. A bear stood at the edge of the forest scratching its belly.

Two men with fishing nets were chasing Julie through the jungle.

Somehow the moon shines. Below it is the city. Barbara stops to tell a cop she's been raped he says sure go home get some sleep honey she slaps him he grabs his face. There, in front of the slow turning windmill, something happened. Nobody around here will talk about it.

Screaming she threw herself on the mercy of the court.

I'm still trying to hitch a ride the only thing going my way is an elephant.

There's the red schoolhouse. TV antennas decorate its roof. The children inside watching the Ed Sullivan Show. Ten thousand chubby boys from Canada singing the Canadian National Blues. The teacher is in the toilet taking a crap.

All the cars are still going to New Jersey. The effect is aggressive. Little people are in each car. You can see their heads.

On the lighthouse hill there is the usual lighthouse and a house that sits back away from it. The sky is overcast. The other hills roll in a symphony of brown and green grass. Scratch the symphony. All the shadows right now fall on this side but you wouldn't believe what happens in the morning you have to be here. All the doors the windows are closed tight. Strange. There are lighthouses all along the way. The sky is big clear open innocent. It can be morning or afternoon or evening the sky is still big open clear, grass along the hillsides is burned sometimes burned red brown black. The lighthouse there the white one with a black dome is the only one without wings and eyes. The others fly away at night.

Sheep houses line the northwest countryside. Except sheep are not kept in them. The first at the fork is occupied by Barbara and Nikki who are stuck together, having merged while dancing during the celebration. In the next five houses live a wild plant, a Buick car, a couple of giant bugs, eleven elves and a gay goblin. The nightwatchman says holy Leda bring back the sheep!

A giant bird with the head of Elmer Blake is eating a naked man. The pink legs dangle from Blake's mouth. The bird is chained to a large platform controlled by tiny workmen.

They constantly fork "sinners" through the back and feed them to Blake who chews them like apples crunch crunch.

Roslyn and Julie have accidentally bumped into each other in front of Inlet's Macy's. As we focus in on them they are in the middle of a violent verbal confrontation. Paul Revere, American patriot and silversmith, colonial agitator, is riding toward them determined to forestall what is likely to turn into a bloody battle. Meanwhile Julie is screaming in Roslyn's face: You dirty no good lobster you goose you olive oil you dried earthworm you pumpkin you soybean you squash. Also meanwhile Roslyn is screaming in Julie's face: You tofu fruit whip you cottonseed crisp you crunchy cricket you rutabaga! As Mr. Revere arrives the two women are thrown off balance by the flurry his horse causes trying to stop. A crowd has gathered and cops are approaching. Even Carter Glass from Lynchburg is there trying to see what's going on. The two women lift themselves from the ground and snatch Revere from his horse and horsewhip him within an inch of his life. Let that be a lesson to you says Julie. After this Roslyn disappears in the crowd.

Al turned and looked up. It was Deborah and Deborah was smiling down at him. Now she started slowly working her fingers into the muscles of his shoulders. It felt good. Oh, yes, Very good. He glanced out of the sides of his eyes just like a character in a novel by a commercial writer. Julie was still down there on the raft. Al saw himself with Deborah in the bedroom, one of the rooms back there. He also saw Jim approaching. He had to hurry. Deborah's hands were strong. The slow, sturdy massaging of the tight muscles that pull tensely from the shoulders to the neck relaxed him and put him at ease. Usually talkative, Deborah was now quiet. He looked up again and saw that she was reading Julie's diary, on his lap. A spasm went through his body. Hello body. But he made no effort to close the thing. Rather he closed his eyes and gave himself to the motion of Deborah's hands. The goodness spread up through his neck to his brain and down his arms. He felt nice and sleepy.

With the green blanket and a white basket of fresh sandwiches and a dark red bottle of Italian wine Julie and Al set out. The world was yet undiscovered.

They picked their way down the narrow path, barefoot, under the tall trees. It was cool. The trees held so much moisture. Yet it was a hot day. The dog was with them.

To the left: *I love you,* painted on a large smooth rock. Beneath it: *I love you too.*

Poot ran ahead and dashed into the gentle crest of waves and began paddling out.

Al stood awkwardly on the foreshore as Julie stood

111

ankledeep in the sunwarmed surf untying the yellow aluminum canoe.

Al walks out onto the dyke and gingerly gets into the water unaware that Julie is watching his daintiness with resentment. Sissy. Meanwhile Poot turns and paddles back toward them and when she is close enough she jumps up onto the dyke and furiously shakes herself. Ah fuck, says Al.

Tiny: a naked girl small and lovely is sunbathing on the other side. She has this habit of attracting birds. Al watches birds diving down to her. They are graceful.

Julie was laughing at Al trying to shield himself from the flying water. Al waded over to the canoe and Julie said, Pick it up so the bottom won't scrape the rocks and she herself took one side and Al the other.

In the canoe was an orange lifesaver. Kneedeep now, Al stopped to strap the thing around his chest. Julie said, Poot, you go back home! Get! She splashed water at the dog on the dyke. The dog gave a brief sheepish look but after a frisky turning about she jumped back into the water and swam over to Julie. Little ugly mut! Goddamnit, fucking Poot, get out! shouted Julie. She pushed the dog out of the canoe and they continued to move out across the smooth water. The morning was still crisp and cool from night air and a far away motorboat was sending its breakers toward them, rocking them. Poot continued to follow, paddling for all she was worth. Finally Al said, You're going to have to take her up to the house and lock her in. Julie's face turned red with anger. For a moment Al thought she would cry. They sat there still, except for the gentle swaying of the canoe. The oars now also still and Poot again was trying to climb into the canoe. Julie snatched the dog up in her arms and leaped out splashing shoulderdeep through the water. She walked holding the wiggling animal out of the lake and up the path to the house and Al sat there unable to know whether he wanted to cry or vomit. He watched the ripples and waited.

everybody in town will have something to say about this situation discontinuous as it is and dangerous even gutbucket low full of tricksters and hot mamas and cool cats and squares and dittybops they'll speak out on the mythopoeic reality of true fiction watch and we'll get 'em all together in the Beulah Railway Station's waiting room and let 'em have their say just before we put 'em on the train for good they'll explain it all all the connections or hand it back to us saying so what and I can just see Mr. Coonshine and Mr. Kneebone with a mouth full of Beckett and Borges talking it out and spitting grape seeds in the grass

hi reader Jim here again our narrator is showing how silly he can be he's never heard Inlet's Jubilee Beaters imitating the Cotton Blossom Singers and the Hampton Colored Students and he certainly never sang from my grandma's *Negro Singers' Own Book* of 1846 so when he says somebody with a gutbucket view of life can explain or eat narrative energy put on a page by say Patchen he's clearly out of touch with say Leadbelly's Becky Dean or the Little Albert Black Magic Book or the Prince Ali Lucky Star Dream Book which interprets dreams in three numbers

"How do you say in English?"

I used to send my wife out into the woods when she bled. Today?

I'm watching my weight. I weigh one thousand sixty-nine pounds.

A blue car passes it is filled with Roslyn taking a steambath.

The road is muddy the trees are wet the houses are all locked for the winter nobody lives back here till summer.

The shipbuilders company is near the graveyard below it at the base of the hill on the Sound it sits there like a crayon drawing by a brilliant child nobody understands. I wish I could say *that* so somebody understands.

Drilling hammering burning sizzling. Thirteen doorways huge steel frames they slide back into walls trucks are driven in and out deep in summer nights while wives are sleeping dreaming world war two or while welded flesh hangs together down the sides of cold ships waiting to leave forever. Trucks from Waterbury arrive daily.

Truck drivers cargo captains on Friday nights in doorways face the yard gamble drink Budweiser talk shoot crap feel the words glued to the latest piece of ass in town.

The lobstermen rig lobster pots repair them too. From the nearby fish-processing plant they get fish remnants for bait the wooden traps work lobsters sail right in.

Jim and other large men get trapped in nylon nets nights while sleeping.

Faces lined with wind rain and sun shield sensibilities as smooth and useful as the pots inside the surface is cool and damp.

Cap shades eyes. Red plaid shirts. Crow's-feet at edges of eyes. They go out leapfrog return go out they count and weigh the years according to the creases in their hands.

A storm at midnight lightning cracking the sky Frankenstein falling out of a high window into leaping flames Dali, or somebody like Dali, coming up the road with a melting clock past a giant skullbone. Naked Julie and Deborah dash out of the underbrush scattering screaming it's an emergency, the system is working sirens all over. Airplanes land to catch their breath to get in and out of the rain trains stop to scratch their confused brows. Naked Deborah is caught suddenly in a large metal walking-contraption. She is giggling like a hyena spots break out over her arms and legs as she struggles to free herself. When she's free she gallops off like a zebra. Yuk.

Because of Jim's fondness for politics and baseball and people of unimpeachable integrity he went to see Judge Landis formally known as Kenesaw Mountain Landis originally from Millville, Ohio. Jim was desperately hurting for advice on his troubled marriage and he figured Judge Landis was about the smartest man in town. Landis also had a good legal mind. The judge's servant let Jim in. The judge and Jim ended up talking about the good old days when the judge was baseball commissioner so they never got around to discussing Jim's problem. Jim left puzzling over his own stupidity. I could kick myself.

The African is in a railroad yard outside of town looking for the meaning of Black Friday. He thinks he sees a hard looking man with a hugh dark beard coming up the tracks. The man is dressed well and looks mean. His hair is thin on the top and his eyes glitter. The man stops in front of The African. He says, Who are you I'm Jay Gould. The African tells Gould about his efforts to find Black Friday. This is one of the rare occasions on which Gould ever laughs. He slaps the African on the shoulder and says, You're a gold mine of humor! The African feels uneasy because he does not understand the joke. Gould walks away laughing to himself and shaking his head.

It doesn't take very long to cross the lake. You head for Little Duck Pond which connects with Duck Pond by way of a narrow river. Al worked one oar and Julie the other. The sky was clearing and the sun moved rapidly overhead. And it was a fresh clean-smelling morning. The wind was gentle and the currents were therefore easy. The flat greenblue surface reflected only a few patches of harmless clouds way overhead. Al and Julie were gliding across now into the low river. *It was like a reflection: a perfect illusion.* Their strokes were smooth and even. Way off to the left on land someone was hammering on wood. The rhythmic slap of the oars was pleasant, naturally. The perfect illusion. They sat facing each other and Julie's eyes were focused sharply on Al. How'd you feel. Fine he said. She searched his face for fear. Don't worry about anything, Al, this canoe won't turn over unless it's forced. A nervous chuckle. I'm not worried. And Julie smiled. Al, why do you suppose you can't swim. I don't know—maybe I got thrown in deep water when I was a kid. Julie smiled the smile she used when she wanted to be superior. Anyway, with the lifesaver, she said, you're safe. I mean if something does happen, which is unlikely. He looked annoyed. Just like a character in straight illusionistic fiction. I told you Julie, I'm okay. I believe you. Not far from the mouth of the river a man wearing a red cap and a blue plaid shirt sat quietly in a silver rowboat, his fishing line lingering calmly in the water. Now the narrow low waterway was crowded on both sides by an awesome profusion of trees and shrubs and their twigs buds seed tassels floated on the moving water around them. Around rocks and beneath vines growing out from the riverbed which in this shallow area was so clear you could see every

inch of its bottom complete with beer cans, ancient rock
and soggy wood. Then after almost scraping bottom they
swerved out into the brightness of Little Duck Pond which
was really a big round lake though not quite as large as
Duck Pond itself. It too was flat and calm and surrounded
on all sides by tall brown heartwood with red-tinged yellow
birch farther back in the moisture of the shade. Now the
sun at this moment made an intense appearance turning
the lake into a glowing bowl of green and blue chips of
expensive glass. In the middle of the lake was a small island
where a single shrub stood like a dead upright sentry. They
kept moving straight across. Julie had a clear idea where
she wanted them to land. She kept pointing toward it. She
knew the area. When they reached it they pulled one end of
the canoe up between two rocks near the edge of the lake at
the foot of a rocky cliff studded with an abundance of
ravines hemlock and moosewood and Julie pointed out
toward the other side farther down where the lake
narrowed again into another river. That's an old fur
trapper's cabin down there can you see it it's been there
since the 1920's some of the kids around here now use it as
a place to make out Rose Marie my cousin whom you'll
meet later on this summer goes there with the local white
boys she's fifteen oh God how she reminds me of myself
when I was fifteen it's disgusting you know Queen of the
Lake the whole bit. Julie laughed. They were now climbing
the loose rocky path and a squirrel dashed through the dry
leaves and underbrush. At a small clearing ahead of them
the squirrel stuck its head out and looked at them, wiggling
its big tail, then with . . .

    With even faster speed, disappeared in the thicket,
rattling twigs humus seedling sprouts and the fallen things
of wintergreen. Now they sat the food and the chianti to the
side and together spread the green fluffy blanket in a
clearing near the edge of the cliff. Julie stripped as Al
found his way out of his lifesaver. They sat down and
kissed. Why're you keeping on your swimsuit. He stood up

and instantly took it off. On his knees he kissed her again. She gave him her tongue. She pulled away and uncorked the wine. Cheerfully she said, Let's have a little wine then take a nap first okay. Here she goes again trying to run the show. Al only sipped the wine and did not respond. Soon Julie recorked the bottle and returned it to the basket with the sandwiches. Lying side by side they couldn't sleep. They hugged and holding each other they kissed then with his erection he entered and moved up into her dampness feeling the warmth of her surround him. Did you come. No I don't have to always come why do you ask me that I don't like it when you ask me that. Sorry, Julie. He got up. I'm going for a walk.

To smell the leaves and put his feet and hands down into the cool water. To listen to the chirp of birds. All so strange. Harlem was never like this. Now from the cliff the water looked like metal and the canoe, pushed by the breeze was knocking against the rocks. A bird saying twickle twickle twickle then twickle twickle. And again.

Al sees coming this way from the mouth of the river a motorboat. Hears its constant groan. White people pink faces. He steps behind a bush suddenly conscious of his nakedness. They see the canoe they know someone's here. Go on by fuckers go on by. The squirrel appears again gazes at Al then runs away again. Meanwhile the boat is closer now and it contains two white men and one is holding a shotgun. They are headed this way. They obviously see the canoe. Nosey. Al squats behind the bush. At the moment they are passing the one with the rifle stands up. The motor is idling. He aims the gun at the bush where Al is hiding and pulls the trigger. The sound CRACK echoes through the woods: *ack ack ack ack ack!* Al rolls over and falls behind a cluster of old stumps and underbrush. Meanwhile scratched and bleeding on the left arm and left thigh, Al feels a huge mixture of rage fear and shame as he crawls back away from the cliff and the bush toward the clearing where Julie apparently is asleep. Like a character in a Richard Wright story he did not think intellectually about what had just happened he just continued to crawl back. For any writer he would be a very predictable and obedient character. He feels silly and angry and ashamed of his fear and reluctant to return to Julie till he can control what he is feeling.

Julie says, What was that.

Shot.

Her eyes grew bigger. A gunshot somebody hunting.

No a white man in a motorboat tried to kill me.

You're kidding.

I wish I were.

Julie's mouth hung opened in disbelief. Al are you absolutely sure.

Sure I'm sure.

I just can't believe that, Al.

You can't believe it because you're too white yourself. And the minute he said it he knew it was the beginning of their separation. Happy bitter day!

Julie picked up her swimsuit and began putting it on. She kept her eyes away from his.

The news is always breaking the record: record-breaking news: man carries woman across threshold six hundred and thirty-two times in two days. (It has been reported that hundreds of people are developing hernias cramps sprains of the ankles and wrists and other types of injuries.)

The man who killed your dog is killed by you. You don't remember it but you murdered the man stabbed him with a Russian dagger left the weapon standing in his chest the sun was shining a tree nearby a boy walking in the park everything except your deed was normal. I'm watching the whole scene from my window.

There I am standing at the doorway of my jet waving to the cameras about to enter the aircraft. My flightcrew smiles with boredom. It's a cloudy day at Kennedy.

My teeth are broken my words they are in another language I am a stranger here unable to speak.

A fat man in undershirt who makes pots sticks his hands into my mouth to try to help me find my way. His fingers touch the inner darkness and this causes his shoe strings to fall off his shoes. A cigarette stuck at the top of his right ear vanishes.

The church bell rings it is in the bell tower across the street gothic windows with ribs and bars. He opens his bottle of beer and says it's six o'clock forget about language have a drink.

121

I take him up on his offer as the children from the school bus wave at us getting drunk and happy.

Julie and many elegant Madison Avenue type Black women in long peasant dresses are coming through the open doorway to join the party. Dudes in expensive jump-suits and short leather jackets. They all talk long distance talk. They stand in corridors and whisper clichés and drop words straight out of the Pocket Thesaurus. When something hits their funnybone their beautiful laughter echoes across the threshold throughout the building from the basement mopcloset to the beachchairs on the roof!

Al had warts. He killed a cat and put it into a supermarket shopping bag along with a transistor radio turned full blast he then went out to the edge of town and buried an afro-comb in black dirt stole a chicken from a chicken shack rung its neck cleaned it and buried it the burial took place at a busy intersection then he went out and found a pig pen he got in it and did it to one of the pigs and being the sort of person he was left a quarter in the pig's rear end. Tied a knot in his own shirt sleeves left his shirt in the graveyard. Invaded a group of boys shooting marbles counted out as many as there were warts on his body tied the marbles in a snotrag threw it in the river waited ten days and was cured.

You are a successful young woman named Roslyn in an expensive pink nightgown stretched out on a lumpy dark bed. In your right hand is an empty gin bottle. One pink shoe on the floor on the right the other on the foot of the bed. Walls are blank and no furniture empty fireplace no rug. You've been here seven days and seven nights.

Oscar and the boys stole a school bus painted, "Fuck You," on it and drove out to the airport to watch the airplanes come in. Nobody crashed everybody got high and higher stars filled the sky. Finished with their joy ride they parked the thing in front of the door to the colored Baptist Church on James Brown Street.

Gimmick is trying to find a more secure footing in this world. No one wants to give him tenure. He's nervous about promotion. He whines. Telling jokes hasn't worked. (He told some pretty good jokes but they didn't do the trick. Things like: a bird in the hand is often messy; last sperm in the hole is a rotten egg; "and prively he caughte hir by the queynte"; war is the cause of chromosome damage; "Jesus Saves?—He didn't even have a job how could he save anything?")

The African is in the Inlet Supermarket shopping for something to eat. It's not easy. American good tastes terrible. He hasn't been able to find food he likes. He's desperate and he's lost weight.

Deborah Ingram, a married woman with whom he had a brief affair, was the only American, so far, who understood his problem and cooked food—on his stove—that he could eat. But he hadn't seen Deborah in a year.

His colleagues at the college were not friendly. He did not understand their lack of friendliness. Yet he was lucky to have the assistant professorship and he meant to keep it.

With his silver metal shopping cart he explored the rows and rows of packaged and processed food items. The place was glossy and bright. Crowded with other shoppers: Cynthia-Carol and Herb, She and He, the Blakes, Gertrude Douglas and Charles Douglas, and seventy-one others. None of them were having the problems the African had. The African kept seeing people loaded down. Some had blue hair and carts loaded with dog food and lemon juice. What was going on in the world that there was such a need for dog food and lemon juice?

Maybe he'd just settle for peanut butter or cans of frog legs. Canned goods and still life.

The kosher butcher was behind the counter waiting to help him. The African took a number and waited while watching the fish and meat in the display-freezer. A cluster of housewives surrounded him. He felt at home among these women. He liked the way they smelled. "Yes sir?" said the butcher and the African spoke. The minute he spoke the housewives smiled and gravitated toward him. The minute it was clear that he was exotic and not an American

Black they got excited and friendly. The loved him as much as he loved them. The housewives offered to help him shop. They advised him on the quality of the meat and fish. He was accustomed to this and expected it here at the meat counter. The butcher was also helpful. "Try the salmon, it hasn't been frozen." So the African bought a small piece of salmon. He gave the butcher his number. It was a forty-three designed by a man named Steve. You could even move it around and change it to thirty-four.

The African puzzled over what else to buy. The potato salad the salad the purple beef tongue the wide display of European cheeses. These were not daydreams he could easily wash out of his mouth once the sting of them touched his taste buds. Pretty soon something had to give.

Even the toilet paper was an unfriendly item but he bought it anyway. Inlet Toliet Paper Company. He bought the unscented kind.

With the salmon and toilet paper and a few other dubious items he went to the checkout counter. The checkout girl was a blonde. He liked blondes but this one was wearing a dull purple Cause on her face and her underskin was clogged with dry patches. Yet he said hello as usual and as usual she refused to return the greeting. She disliked her job and hated all customers. They got on her nerves. She rung up his stuff and bagged it and turned her attention to the lady behind the African.

When the African reached the doors they opened on their own for him. He felt like a king stepping out into the sunlight equipped with his salmon and toilet paper. What could possibly go wrong?

Jim and Deborah sat on a rock facing The Sound. They were silent for a long time then Deborah spoke:

"Fqjbv xzsapol dkjwqr bhsl. Dcyrplaz but Christ I ghkwq hjgrtyui so much kwqazxcv!"

"Rkhqwopsa hjg brpo vrpi crjw fdssazo namluoo nuwery."

"I know, oh jureqaz. Cadrut cupsaj mazxq fuppo kulwexz."

Jim smirked. "Huuyxsawqmnblgh then, of course, hsaderwqxz and who knows tyuiojhgkecbvn ghj fde."

"Utrio kgf."

"Dsazx qwe."

Deborah brushed her silky hair back from her face. "My mother hgdsapo rytumo fgkd vwqa."

Jim touched her hand. "I guuhb."

"Usurh."

"Burmph soc."

"Szax nabvmp."

"Defc . . ." He stopped. A tear rolled down his cheek. "Pupifh but it's khgbvcxw—*don't you see?*"

He put his arm around her and she put hers around him and they rocked each other.

A barge was going by it said BOOOOOOOOOOOOO OOOOOOOOOG then again BOOOOOOOOOOOOOO OOG and again BOOOOOOOOOOOOOOOOOOOOOO OOG.

Rose Marie Blake small and lovely with blond hair is lying on her back one leg drawn up so that her foot is close against her buttocks the other is held up. A raven is perched on the toes of this foot. Holding it firmly with both hands she feeds an apple to the raven. It pecks. Pecks again. Looks around. Pecks twice. Looks. Pecks again. Looks. Broken whiskey bottles are all around her.

She has this habit of attracting birds. They like her odor. They come to her and curiously chirp, Let me in let me in let me in let me in let me in let me in let me . . .

Hourari was on the beach wandering around. The sand was still damp from the storm during the night. Debris: rotten oranges cigarette butts egg shells pop bottles candy wrappers. The sun was pink coming up a dead hawk stuck in the sand, its head rammed into a soggy grapefruit rind. He ran his naked toe into the earth and felt its juices. At that hour in the morning the ocean was calm the sky was calm the house back there was quiet everybody still sleeping. The sun suddenly stopped. It began to melt. He couldn't believe his eyes. The hawk at his feet began to shake itself. The sun suddenly disappeared that's when the rain came and he ran toward the house with the sound of the bird crying for help.

"The door to the oven is hot. I open it. I take one side my wife the other. Together we life the stuffed onions out. Smells good. Are you coming to dinner?"

The buildings have all fallen in on each other. Years ago

opposing groups of experts warned against this. Windows doors door mats and eyes mouths thresholds all rubble piles of structure, form, and across the street Jim Ingram sits in a restaurant with his back to it all even the people out here in the rain carrying umbrellas. His brother is in the hospital he cut off his finger. He won't talk to me keeps whispering to himself. I take a train to the all-night cafe to see if I can dig up somebody who cares about what is happening. The lighted backroom shows through the open doorway. A man at the edge of town is whistling on a bridge watching a boat arrive. I can't stand the lack of concern so I go south to watch people from the open window built in 1905 to show the beach and the ocean.

I pushed the furniture against the door piled the logs against the furniture. Whatever it was it was still out there. I refuse to be dragged out or fed or loved or tortured. I push the people, the short fat man the tall skinny girl the wide flat woman the thin ugly girl, against the whole pile of stuff. I think I'm safe in here. No one is strong enough to move all this stuff, all these people. I take the bear by his ear and throw him on the pile. He groans. The door is no longer visible . . .

Let me count the ways.

1. The man who shot at Al was, a) Captain Delano, b) Ahab, c) you, d) The Neighbor Obstinate, e) the person who found a ship while deep sea diving, f) Paul while taking a break from painting the Great Tree.

2. The Doorway of Life, when opened, will bleed or it will not bleed.

3. There is a stage with a partition down the center. In effect: two rooms separated by a wall. A door—presently locked—opens from the left room into the right. There is a character moaning and crying on the right side. On the left another character is jumping up and down screaming and beating his fists against his thighs. Which way is best?

4. Again, Barry beat his fist on the table. What is the rest . . . ?

5. He did *not* necessarily think he was learning to know her well.

6. Can the threshold exist outside the context of the doorway?

7. What would you do in a *real* emergency? Break the glass and pull the handle?

Al is standing naked in the little house looking through the screen as the blue Mustang hardtop pulls up and parks. A boy and a girl get out. First to come down the path is the girl. She has a pumpkin face with large stone-gray eyes. Chestnut hair parted down the middle hanging to the shoulders. White blouse dark green pants. A realistic girl. Sandals with straps across the instep. A very realistic person. At a distance she looks white, closer she is obviously colored: full lips and something else that can't be described. Or shown. Second comes the boy with a stack of records under his right arm. The fact that they are under his right arm qualifies him for total realism. With Al watching them approach it is a totally realistic situation. Under the other arm the boy is carrying a bundle of blankets. He is tall and skinny with long shaggy hair. He also sports a beard. He wears a colorful Indian shirt and bell bottoms and like the girl he's wearing sandals. These two minor characters seem more realistic than the other characters because of the way they come on. Nobody for example has noticed the color of *Julie's* hair. What is this—some kind of discrimination?

Meanwhile Poot runs out to meet the new arrivals and when she stops barking she sniffs them and wags her tail for them. And when they stop at the steps she licks their toes. All of this, dear reader or listener, is still from Al's point of view. Now Al can hear Barbara and her best friend Nikki on the deck greeting the boy and the girl. At this point Al touches Julie with his foot. And she turns over in her sleep away from him. He is standing on the mattress only a few inches from her. He's now looking down at her. Let her sleep. But she's waking. What time is it. It's getting late. Now he looks through the screen again, realistically. Action. Dialogue. The whole bit. Julie stretches her arms and yawns. Already I hate that fucking job. She stretches her legs under the cover. I took the job at the Corked Pussy Cat because I thought I couldn't stand it up here otherwise. I mean just being out here in the country and not going any place can be a drag. Julie is speaking with her eyes closed. The tips aren't anything like what I thought they'd be. Al sat down beside her. He looked at her. I don't like her now. I think your cousins just arrived. Julie's eyes open and stretch. Rose Marie and Patrick she says. I guess so. A blue Mustang. Julie stands up and looks through the screen. She's rubbing her eyes. A beautiful bitch says Al to himself. Real. A realistic reflection. Golden pink body in soft afternoon light. Peach fuzz. Peachy. Julie yawns again stretching her arms above her head. This means that tomorrow on Sunday my uncle and aunt will get here they'll probably stay only a few days she has this very rigid job you see and Gloria their other daughter the one who's paralyzed remember I told you about her she will be with them she's nice Gloria I mean. She looks at Al for the first time since waking. I think you'll like her I know she will like you. At this moment a car goes by on the road, realistically, driven by a fat white man wearing an army garrison hat. A small boy and a small girl are in the back seat playing. King Lear asks Albany to undo a button at a moment when tragedy and grief have just about wiped him out. What is the meaning of the monkey in O'Connor's "A Good Man is Hard To Find"? Only Al notices the car going by and since the realistic reader is supposed to see—at this point at least—what he sees, and assumes it's relevant, the reader or viewer must also assume that the passing car has meaning. At the same time one should not be surprised if neither the car nor the garrison hat nor the children nor the man turn up again. But a royal battle—that's a different ball game.

Julie is always grouchy for the first hour or so after

waking so Al goes out on the deck and sits in a chair with his feet on the rail. Blasting from the loudspeaker attached to outside of the bighouse is a gutsy vocal and instrumental composition. Al closes his eyes and wonders how he got so far from Harlem and what ever happened to the kinds of Black people he always knew.

Al and Julie went for a walk along one of the trails in the nearby woods. When the path was wide enough they walked side by side. Otherwise Julie took the lead.

"................." said Julie.

"..............."

She looked at him. "But..................................."

He avoided her eyes. "................"

A twig snapped somewhere.

"I own the Patchquilt Store I make quilts out of scraps silk cotton nylon rayon synthetics you name it. My wife is mostly interested in automobiles she repairs them changes the oil for thousands of motorists, me, I spend my days here in the back room sewing little squares, these things, of bright cloth together. My door is always open and my prices are reasonable."

Beautiful but dangerous tigers roam around the edges of my life. I see them prowling and tracking down sheep squirrel and deer it's a mess. It is no rumor: more tigers are coming all the time.

The wild man with skin as tough as the bark of a tree runs deep into the forest when he sees people. I found one of his fangs and some of his thick white hair. People on the outskirts say his name is Jim.

On the outskirts of town when a man carried his hoe into the house he died instantly. His doorway gave no warning. Folks called him Elmer.

Alla Blake had rheumatism. She filled her pillow with fresh hops and was completely cured the next morning. It's a miracle.

The horse that broke out of the barn down the road was found dead late the next afternoon. No one believed that a witch had rode it to death.

Roslyn reached for a broom leaning against a wall. It fell to the floor. Two hours later she almost died.

Years ago Barbara yawned during church service. She was invaded by the devil who twisted her heart into a knot and held it till it almost stopped beating.

This sixty-nine year old American of Watusi ancestry married an eighteen year old of Korean ancestry they slept together and the older one got strong as a California oak and the younger one got so weak he or she died a sad helpless death.

Janice Page with a lung infection ate twenty pounds of raw onions and was cured.

Jim Ingram with a liver infection ate only liver and miracle of miracles, he was cured forever. When he continued to eat liver though he almost died.

When the kids come in the house Jim will go out and fix the boat.

Barbara is sedate and shy she wears everything everybody ever told her on her face, a long purple dress she has dimples.

Jim has handy man equipment cement stuff he bought in town he's fifty. Wears a dirty cap.

Deborah is grinning she holds on to the railing that leads to the door they're in the yard. The children are coming in soon..

Jomo is a devil man who sucks a snake deep into his belly. His feet are claws his breasts are like a woman's.

They're coming in soon. The children I mean.

Hourari's horns are made of red and green feathers his eyes are empty holes flames burn at the back of them. He's the figurehead over a doorway on a sidestreet.

The children enter now. Deborah has understanding and bold grief. The children smooch to the rock music then turn the records over.

Jim's out there now fixing the boat. "Let us lower our heads in prayer."

A SELECTION OF NAMES FROM THE
INLET TELEPHONE DIRECTORY

Eagle Wing
Zudie O
Sandy Ree Georgia
Cotton Eyed Joe
Scip
Br'er Rabbit
Railroad Boy
Baby Child Brown
Cornshuck Henry
Harp Playing David
Marengo
Mr. Bullfarte
Rock Candy
Hampton Sue
Banjo Tucker
Mr. Nobody
Conjer Man
Medicine Man
Bandana Attucks
Joseph Lubin
Dart Hobler
Rosemarie Page
Kishiko
Mack Burt
Becky Dean

Banjo X
Daddy
Miss Sue Cum
Hobble Skirt Mary
Stepback Sally
Cocaine Snookyjump
Crackerjack Rex
Jubilee Beater
Alex Roots
Miss Anne White
Mr. Moneyfoot Rooster
Mr. Taters Fox
Cherokee Susan
Joe X Clark
Titanic Henry
Monkeywoman Mae
X-ray Dress Sally
Pharoah Black
Eva Seno Jaffe
Carlo Woolf
Priscilla Worth
Miss Justa B. Minute
Gerda
Katya Barnes
Jessica Cott
Romanticist Buckwheat

Miss Little Bingo
Pensacola Bill
Gravey
Sop
Coonshine Joe
Mr. Kneebone Hide
Squirrel Lack
Rolling Pin Jekyll
Hogfat Sam
Woodpecker Grum
Revivalist Simmons
Ella Speed
Daddy Jim
Gospel Train Jane
Beulah
Cotton Blossom Fern
Andy
Amos
Black Magic Man
Lizabet the Witch
Mythmaker Bill
Classicist Charlie
Independence Mack
Swamp Man
Backdoor Man

Emergency numbers: fire police sheriff state patrol emergencies and accidents doctor home ambulance U.S. Secret Service Poison Center. Inlet Emergency Call Warning: it is against the law to interfere with a person trying to report an emergency. Report all annoyances improper language and malicious calls. Keep a handy list of the telephone numbers for the Connecticut Bureau of Investigation the Connecticut State Patrol the Road Condition Information Service the Non-Emergency Duty Officer Military Police Drug Enforcement Administration and the County Ambulance Dispatch. In metro areas only dial operator. In case of extreme emergencies call (as loudly as you can) 911.

Naturalism is supposed to be scientific, objective and in the American tradition. Here goes your naturalism: Naked, Al Julie and Barbara went swimming in the moonlight. Nikki Rose Marie and Patrick were in the bighouse playing cards. Al of course was not swimming since he couldn't but he was playing around in the water. Trying to screw Julie. And Barbara was splashing water on them and laughing at them. Such a rare moment of happiness for the fat girl. At this moment they heard a car drive up and stop. Barbara had the answer: That must be Uncle Blake and Aunt Alla and Gloria. You know we should go up and say hello or something. Julie agreed. Naturalistically, they dried themselves put on their clothes and went up and Barbara joined the card game after greeting her relatives. Introducing Al, Julie made a big fuss over him, nervously. Knowing how prudish her uncle was. She deliberately rubbed it in hoping it would hurt his soul yes his soul. Such a stupid nonentity word. No meaning but Julie's uncle deserved the word he was just a tightass snob. He lost years of sleep worrying about the morality of people who fucked before marriage. Mr. Blake left the room. A light complexioned man with reddish hair freckles and gray eyes, he wore slacks and a sport shirt, in the naturalistic tradition. Al of course serves us as the point-of-view. He also noticed Mrs. Blake: also light, fat and short: resigned and exhausted, a person who spent all her free time in the kitchen wiping the stove or searching for grease spots. She was doing that now in the kitchenette visible from where the others gathered in the family room. She was capable of inspiring pathos. Gloria sat in her wheelchair pretty with a pear-shaped face large clear tan eyes and a huge afro that stood up red and stiff like a royal crown. She could wobble around a bit with braces on her legs and crutches under her arms but mostly she remained in the chair. Al watched her with interest. She watched him with interest. Julie noticed this and was pleased. Julie went over and pushed Gloria's chair closer to Al. The lamplight, naturalistically, glowed from Gloria's clear steel-rimmed eyeglasses. Her eyes behind them were large and wet. They were always damp and sad. Her mouth also had a wet look. Mrs. Blake finished wiping the stove and stood awkwardly in the space between the kitchenette and family room. Using good timing, Mr. Blake returned at that moment and announced that his wife and he were tired and therefore were about to go to bed. Gloria he said are you cold. No, Dad. Elmar Blake obviously was not pleased with this answer. He frowned. He obviously tried to think of something else to say. Obviously for the moment he could not think of anything else to say so he turned and left the room. Julie gave Al what is known in naturalistic literature as a knowing look. He gave it back to her. It was a hot potato. Some characters refuse to hold hot potatoes. At this point Gloria turned back to Al. How's the weather in Harlem. The question confused Al. He finally got an answer to her: I grew up there and I lived in Harlem for a long time but I moved. Oh? What do you do? she asked. Do? he said. I do uh I do uh what do you mean what do I do? Al was aware that he could not tell this proper, chair-ridden lovely young woman that he normally sold drugs for a living. He said: I have a private business, investments. She smirked. He grinned and Barbara coughed. Julie sneezed and said, Excuse me. At this point Mr. Blake returned and said, Gloria, dear, don't you think you should lie down and take a nap—after that long trip you must be . . . And to Al he said, through a silly grin, You will excuse her won't you Al may I call you Al. Sure. Julie, sitting on the arm of the chair where Al sat, pressed her leg against his arm. The record player stopped and turned itself off. Gloria, in a small voice said Yes Dad.

Deborah and Julie met at Inlet's Yellow Fingers for lunch. Julie was determined not to argue.

"Hugfdswo," said Julie.

"Jkwsaopvcxzwerfg then fghksdaw afd bvc asdfghjkl."

"But my dear thfdsg wedpfaszxmn. Then you must understand that hgfdswpfk bvcsq dfs kjh jhgfyu rewop. Viocp."

Deborah fingered the waiter over. "Bring me a drink. Ughfd. My dear, you see it's ghfqpo fgrewlkj cvrefd bnhr xcews dfg."

"I know."

"Do you really gfdadew."

Julie, who rarely smoked, lit a cigarette. "Mother, listen, I must *talk* with you—we must really learn how to *talk* fdwpolkjhguyt with each other. The reason dfgqwdsa xcqwas zxsa werd fgvh thfe."

I know . . ."

"Do you really know—*really?*"

" . . . ."

Not since James Joyce has reading in the toilet been so interesting. Jim Ingram is downtown and has to shit. He rushes into the police station then into its public toilet. The swinging door swings behind him.

Now he's sitting there pants down around his ankles straining and silently reading the inscriptions on the walls of the booth: "20th October 1883. To-day I was taken to the Provincial Government Board to be certified. Opinions differed. They disputed and finally decided that I was not insane—but they arrived at this decision only because during the examination I did my utmost to restrain myself and not give myself away. —Tolstoy, *The Older Self.*" Jim only half believes the signature. Above this confession: "Read carefully: The emergency brake chart, table 8 on page 8 may save your life." And: "Paradise is not in the Lost and Found."

With ceremony Jim wipes himself. He considers the opposite wall: "Running two different conversations in columns alongside each other has been done. Careful now."

He flushes the toilet and with his birthday ink pen adds to the hall of fame: "This whole experience is a bad joke. No more bad jokes!"

Barbara drank horse piss as a cure for fits was cured and taken down to New York to be examined by medical experts who did not believe . . .

Deborah was badly frostbitten she cured it by having her entire body soaked in cowshit for forty-eight hours.

Gloria Blake had this habit of cracking her knuckles pulling the joints of her fingers till they made that popping sound. They threatened to chop off her arms.

Unmarried Gloria watched men laying cornerstones to the courthouse. Her boyfriend decided not to marry her.

My rented truck broke down half way into the interior, children from the mud huts gathered around till their pressure crushed me.

Jim tried to leap from the roof and was caught in a giant rat trap, lucky only one leg broke.

I crawled out through the bottom by digging a hole deep into the earth then came up near the river where naked workers were climbing trees for mango.

In the distance Egyptians are building pyramids. I'm not thrown by this sort of thing. I walk till I reach forty-second and Broadway, inside a dark cool theatre the natives in India are protesting the building of an English railway system by the hundreds they throw themselves in front of speeding trains.

There were many important persons at Jim's and Deborah's wedding. After the ceremony Deborah sat on the front steps of the church, lifted her gown and scratched her pubic area.

I call my mother to tell her a war is about to start she says don't worry about me worry about yourself. I go searching for myself in manuscripts I gave up on years ago. It's a penetrating process.

Born rich Anki taught herself how to live in herself and how to live with deflated breasts. She holds her orgasm away from her body. She has done this successfully for years. Boys wearing grey masks search for it with flashlights.

Neighbors found Deborah and Julie locked together in the closet where Jim left them. They sat four inches from their own shit. It was like going way off somewhere where you could talk to yourself and not have to hear anybody real respond.

The nightwatchman sits inside a small warm area.

I went home after work my wife was tied to the kitchen chair she had been raped and robbed. There was an old man in the bathtub soaking himself when I asked what the fuck he was doing he smiled sheepishly. Said I'll be done in a minute.

Roslyn and Jim had tea in the garden. Their bodies quivered beneath their clothes. Their clothes were imported from a distant land.

The light bulb inside the barbershop sign burned out ten years ago. The hotel marquee flickers like a broken promise.

Women with thick black pubic hair and tits that have been chewed excessively are dancing in the night club. Thighs heavy and veined. Once they are home sleeping they continue to dance in the dreams of men like Jim Ingram who saw them earlier. This does not mean however that those dancers become eternal.

Allen Morris playing dead in a coffin is dressed better than he ever dressed in life as they lower him into the earth. He thought he was dreaming but he cannot find his way back.

An innocent little girl named Julie goes crazy one morning at the breakfast table: "Shit Fuck piss, eat my doo- doo!" Then she runs from the kitchen.

A scholar once asked me are you trying to write like Barth you know Barth in his stories always sounds like he's teaching a creative writing class I don't like that kind of stuff I think it's misdirected it's just a gimmick. Hello gimmick. Naturally I couldn't answer the scholar's question but it's nice to meet gimmick again.

I introduced gimmick to Deborah.

Hello Deborah. Deborah manages to arrive at the summer place due to the presence of a gimmick. It's called language. But it likes its nickname best: gimmick. Deborah's white 4-door Chevy is parked alongside the road behind Barbara's purple VW. Oscar arrives with Deborah he's a chubby pinkish boy with light hair and light eyes who looks more like James Russell Ingram than his mother. Yellow short sleeve shirt blue pants white tennis shoes. Deborah, dear gimmick, is in a tight white cotton dress. This is a fashion show folks! Only with a gimmick can you have a decent literary fashion show. The two, Oscar and Deborah, are coming down the path toward the house. There is no point-of-view, except you own, to observe them. You have to be the judge. Thanks to the gimmick of language you can take on this responsibility.

Here we go. The birds were out that morning singing in the trees and the sun was already high up and bright. It was clearly going to be a warm pleasant day. Good old gimmick.

Scene in the little house: Julie asleep. Al propped against pillows reading a murder mystery. Al heard Deborah and Oscar arriving but he did not look. Why should he look, what's the point in peeking out everytime somebody arrives. Like a nosey old lady. He hadn't met

Oscar but there was no hurry. He looked at Julie snug in
the fetus position snoring for all she was worth. Due to a
gimmick before he realized it someone was knocking at the
screened door. Hello in there you lovebirds can you stand
company. It was beautiful Deborah. And at the sound of
her mother's voice Julie woke with a grouchy face yawning
and scratching her ass beneath the cover. Al let Deborah in
and though he was wearing only his underwear he was
surprised that he wasn't blushing and that he felt all right
about being almost naked in front of Deborah. Julie was
naked and she came from under the covers and kissed her
mother in the mouth. Deborah cheerfully sat on the edge
of the mattress. Deborah kissed Al. Julie yawned again.
Deborah smelled of expensive perfume thanks to the
gimmick of money. Al and Julie smelled of dry sperm.
Deborah liked the odor better than her own. Oh to be
young again.

Deborah kicked off her shoes and sat with her legs
folded beneath her. Al, she said, you were supposed to lift
me across the threshold does he lift you Julie. No I don't
believe in that communist stuff Mother. Do you ever follow
the rules Al. Deborah it's just a gimmick he said. I think the
politicians in the state of Connecticut are just out to legislate
morality. Well said Deborah that's what the radicals the
communists the Left have always said since the new law
came in but I didn't know you were radical Al. I'm not. I
just got my own mind and my own thoughts about things.
Deborah smiled at what she imagined was his lack of
sophistication. She liked him anyway maybe because he was
not sophisticated. Say have you two lovebirds had breakfast
yet of course you haven't what d'you say we whip up some
eggs and bacon and coffee you have your hot-plate and do
you have eggs? Yes, Mom I'll do it. Julie yawned again and
scratched under her arms. Al was watching Deborah
closely she seemed pinker than usual it was probably the
makeup and there was some sort of blue tint in her hair no
maybe purple but it looked good on her. Julie crawled

across the floor to the tiny refrigerator and took out the carton of eggs and the bacon and a loaf of wheat bread. Deborah said I'll make the coffee while you do that. There was no water supply in the little house so Deborah took the pot over to the bighouse and returned with the coffee and water and plugged it into the wall while Julie scrambled the eggs and bacon in a skillet on the hot-plate. While they waited for the stuff the three of them sat on the mattress facing each other. Deborah placed her arms around them and pulled them to her hugging them as tightly as she could. Listen to me you two lovebirds don't ever let anybody come between you you hear me there's nothing on earth more important than love and loving. Due to the warmth of this gimmick Al felt very moved by the gimmick. Julie who was already familiar with her mother's sentimental nature was not moved at all in fact she was thinking that the bacon might be burning and that it should probably be turned over and due to the gimmick of the word fork she was able to turn each of the six strips of bacon over before any of them burned badly.

I wish I could invite my scholar friend to sit with these three characters and watch them eat their own words, I mean bacon and eggs.

If I could place the scholar there with them he would see Al get up now and go out on the deck leaving his breakfast untouched. Looking at the back of his head Julie says, Aren't you going to eat. He looks so beautiful and strong and black standing there in his white shorts. He does not answer and Julie and Deborah look with raised eyes at each other. Al may not know it but his gimmick is working and he's never been anywhere near a creative writing class.

Excerpt from Police Report

ARRESTS March 1, 19—

George Gale
Brian Cabus
Joseph Burke
Tayna Swartz
Marcelo Tomplin
Amy Gavin
Sami Banjar
Maxine Barnett
Larry Ming
Lois Marvel
Jimmie Marvick
Brett Rawlings
Myron Reed
Margret Ayers
Janice Snow
Elizabeth Bohe
Ruth Kernen
Eric Chambers
Nadine Snyder
Candy Fisher
Margot Rosenthal
Toni Bassman
Carol Smith
Evangeline Spruce
Howard Longman
Lee Junior
Sally Mapleton
Karen Nextdoor
David Cress Jones
Dr. Jean Ronick
Amy Behrens
Clare Gitman
Terry Matthews

Jack Lucero
Alison Plaster Puss
Fannie Mae Brown
Arthur Louisville
Wess Viewman Smith
Depot Jones
Patrick O'Malley
Chris Ondrejka
Daisy Moench
Patricia Boksenbaum
Ethel Queen
Nellie L. Puddle
Michelle Kuteness
Riva G. Pryor
Lora Quick Quick
Sara Neal
John Publicman
Teddy Puff
Ruth Puff
Keith Banks
Red Holmes
Marlyn Hirschfeld
Susan Beeson
Edith Hink
Molly Higgenbottom
Cindy Highassman
Emma Torkin
Jeff Bellhandle
August Rentward
Vicki Arapahoe
Josh Beerward
Judy Stepchile
Gay H. Gathering

The place in the distance wasn't clear. In the morning it will be Jim's tool shed with light falling in brightly against the rotten planks of the wall where a hammer pliers gadgets hang. A large bug also clings to the wall. "Who left the door open?"

The tax collector is a man of few words. "My wife's place is in the home." She scratches at the door of his locked memory. In his dream he can fly but she has to thumb a ride.

Stray wolves chase our hens into the barn.

When I was a kid I searched for Roslyn's orgasm it was always hiding in the back of a locked closet or down in the basement behind the furnace.

Slender Julie in white pants hair tied up covered with yellow scarf, smiling small hands petite bright clear teeth dark eyes long smooth neck bare arms bare shoulders belly bare breasts covered with two red and white scarves tied together around neck. She's carrying a large white threshold over head to shield self from blasting sun. The news in her head is that the preacher who replaced the thresholds of Jade and South Sea pearls at the Holy Ghost Church has again replaced *those* thresholds with Baroque Pearl-Studded thresholds. She walks swiftly along a side street, careful not to upset the thing balanced above. A man in white follows her. He is probably her father. He looks very scientific his hair is cut in the form of a spaceship. He watches her balance. "What would happen, Miss, if you

discovered after my death that I have not been a good
samaritan that the information I sleep with is not my own
what would you do if you knew me."

She goes into the pancake house he sits at the same booth
with her. "What would you do if you knew the Jews started
lifting you across the threshold what would you say, Miss."
While he scratches his name into the table top she eats
potato pancakes.

Alla Blake feeds pigeons in the park they eat out of her
hands. She talks to them they ride her shoulders and arms
even the top of her head.

Deborah teaches Oscar how to knit she does not want him
to grow up to be like other men. They sit on the front porch
knitting together. The dog sleeps at the edge of the porch
the sun is going down.

A bunch of young women work at a joint called The Ritual
of the Foreskin. It's a massage parlor. Across the street the
marquee of a movie house boasts its current feature, The
Punishment of the Uncircumcised next door is a joint called
Glans Removal they sell porno magazines and films Oscar
and other teenage boys loiter around the door till morning.

Jim and Roslyn are sleeping in the woods. Man and
woman. They are unaware of themselves.

Julie slender in a long white dress strolls along the hillside.
Her dark hair is long and stringy she wears a wide hat a
black boy on a donkey follows her.

Alexander Graham Bell called Jim on the telephone. Jim
was excited and therefore nervous as he spoke. Bell sensed
this which caused him to speak softly and reassuringly. It
didn't help, Jim was still nervous. Bell said you know there

is no great secret to this instrument just as there is nothing mysterious about speaking with the deaf. Jim's nervous laughter was followed by this comment: My wife says I have never communicated with her. She says it has been the main problem of our marriage. How can I transmit to her the fact that I am not sure I want to try any more. Bell sighed and said I'm having trouble with Western Union Telegraph Company and I'm not sleeping well. My wife has slept with Africans said Jim. Bell said I never went to Africa. Jim said Bell said Jim said Bell said. Finally Bell said have you heard of this fella named Thomas Alva Edison? What about him. Well said Bell he thinks the electric light bulb's place in the American experience is greater than that of the digressive novel.

He slept beneath the sink where he could smell the dampness.

She entered and left the kitchen countless times during the day.

He could hear her in the front rocking herself in her rocking chair. She sang country songs and did her knitting and ate cottage cheese.

Her motion was a rocking motion she was under the weight of herself.

"Do you believe that . . ."

"It is possible that you may change my life," he said. His face was black. His hands were pink.

Her face was white. Her hands were black. "Yes. I started toilet training early. I'm healthy. I can make a difference."

He kept his eyes closed, knowing that the reality of that moment could not be shifted. He could hear her going and coming. The process of her movements was like Gertrude Stein's fiction. She was in the continuous present.

He was in the past and that was why it was so painful watching her move in the present.

Superior Pussy filled his mailbox with flyers; he was determined to put a stop to the animals that kept dying in his soup.

The day when he could no longer enjoy the dampness, he went to visit James, who lived in a Turkish Bath House. James invited him to go horseback riding through the downtown streets. James, whose father owned the police department, assured him there would be no trouble.

He took the woman with him. James was mad. Said, "Listen, I don't think the woman can come along. This is . . ."

"The imagination runs away like a wild horse."

She watched him scraping mud from his boots. "The kids are hiding under the bed, they too, have imaginations. But yours runs away from you. Your head is in the clouds. It floats up there and it stays up there . . . it is a balloon with a . . ."

"A long way to go, I said you have a long way to go. You have many doors to open before . . ."

"I don't want to argue anymore. I'm sick of this! I want a divorce! I'm going to my mother's, right now."

Julie's friend Sara Neal is here Sara is white, her husband recently divorced her she's unhappy has two small kids and Julie respects her she's no threat.

They drive over to the other side of Inlet to Sara's house. A bright sparkling house white with lime green trimmings. A square house overdone even gaudy. They get out. Julie says, Sara's house was once shown in a magazine. The level of Al's interest is expressed by a grunt.

A young woman is casually turning the pages of a magazine. She's sitting on her back porch. Two visitors arrive. She stands. She is long and bony with huge dark eyes unfriendly eyes. To the left in the yard a little girl plays on a red metal swing. She stops swinging and stares at the visitors. Hi, here we are, says Julie, pushing open the screened door. Al follows. Julie reminds Sara that she's already met Al. Sure says Sara. Yeah says Al.

The little girl speaks, You have perspiration. Al gives her a smile. That's because I'm a big man.

Sara's inspection of Al: sharp polite quick. Julie wants to know the verdict. Sara makes her wait.

My name is Cynthia says the child. She's sitting on Al's lap. I'm Allen. What's your last name. Morris. Mine is Neal Cynthia Neal.

José Cruz a young businessman Sara's boy friend arrives. John F. Kennedy is not expected. Mystery hangs over the whole situation. The recent moon landing has put everyone off. Malcolm X is not expected. So what do you do.

The party: Jim Ingram and Barbara and Nikki arrive and they are soon settled around Sara's big yellow ochre table in the bright dining room. Everyone except Julie and Jim exchange words. *I wish dad would for once reveal himself to me . . . I dreamed last night that he made love to me behind some bushes.*

Julie wants to go downstairs to visit Rosetta the Spanish speaking maid.

Rosetta is not in her room she must be outside watching the moon or she's gone for a walk.

Al and Julie are on her bed. She pulls her panties to the side he unzips and pushes his penis into her vagina and they move awkwardly against each other. She is not enjoying it, he is not enjoying it. He finishes, she does not.

Back upstairs they separate.

Nicholas Zieff. That lovable sad person so lonely and sensitive and brilliant, a brilliant teacher. Nick shits through a mechanical device embedded in his left hip. His normal passage no longer functions. The reader's point of view is important at this moment. The reader sees Nick through a thick cloud of cigarette smoke. Nick is not smoking.

Nick is sliding a cigar in and out of Julie's mouth and Julie is giggling. Al is watching. Others watch.

Al goes to the scotch bottle.

As Nick's thick red hand reaches toward Al's lean black one there is obvious caution. I'm Nick and I guess you're Allen Morris Christ I've heard a lot about you really pleased to see Julie so happy like this really happy for you both, really! She deserves you believe me she's a truly good and beautiful person.

In a far corner Jim Ingram sits brooding.

What's the best word to describe this scene: sentimentality irony romanticism melodrama absurdity.

The Swedish family. Anki Christer and their daughter whose name I forgot. Beautiful girl. Stockholm oh yes Stockholm.

Half of them are dancing to loud dance music. Poor Nick is awkwardly jerking around on the floor too. Everyone feels sympathetic.

Nick is speaking: Anki goddamnit do you realize that in all these years we've known each other I've had but one thought concerning you foremost in my mind . . .

Meanwhile Christer is holding up his drink to somebody saying Salut et fraternité.

Nick: I've always wanted to fuck you Anki and . . .

Anki's eyes nervously flutter. Her pleasant smile disappears. She can't decide whether to be tolerant or offended.

Nick is obviously waiting for a cue. He wants to say it again to make sure she understands. Anki doesn't always understand. The language problem.

The child's name is suddenly remembered: Anita yes Anita. Anita is mad and pretty and determined to defend her mother. Christer seems to turn his back on what is happening. Anita takes over. She says: Nick, listen Nick, you're a nice man but you're awfully crude.

Julie, who is dancing with José, is trying to figure out what is going on. She knows something is happening.

Al is in the toilet sniffing coke.

Nick forces Anki to lie down on the couch and he's now on top of her. He forces her pink knees wide apart. Several men, including Al, take Nick by the shoulders and lift him off Anki. She is red with anger and frustration.

Anki lights a cigarette.

It is Anki herself who is the first to offer Nick comfort. She stands and rests her right hand on his shoulder. Nick it's all right Nick.

He holds his head in his hands and sobs.

Everyone is quiet and watching. The music has stopped.

Nick I'm talking to you, Anki says, I said it's all right.

Jim Ingram touches Nick's shoulder. Come on Nick I'll drive you home. Come on.

Pete Joe Sam Rob Jerry Ron Herb Peggy Sharon May Tony Ruth Sonny Aaron Billy Clarence John and Susan are eating butterfly weed and spinach. Roy Connie Greg and Marcia are eating seed pods with beef cooked gently in elephant garlic gooseberries in goat cream cheese and rhubarb. China Ish and Jed are drinking German beer eating macaroni peppers and okra.

The doctor sharpens his knife. Johnny Hawkins is stretched out on the operating table.

Alla Blake's shoes had holes cut at their toes. The toes stuck out. She sat on a foldup chair against a brick wall.

The family up the road found an infant deer. Front leg broken. It ate all the books in the house. When it went to school with the kids state troopers pulled it inside a car and drove away.

Hourari wiped blood from his hands onto the doorway the dead lamb at his feet had seemed larger a moment ago when it was alive. He drank a handful of its blood. Some of it spilled down his legs to his feet and ran along the wood of the threshold.

It's 1966. A girl's head is framed by a window. That same year the African sees a woman in another window. She's watching a singer sing and a guitar player play. I watch him.

We're inside a farmhouse. Soon we will visit somebody in a

bedroom. Anki in bed watching through an open window a train going by.

In the distance José Cruz heard rumbling like an earthquake sounded like eight point nine on the Gutenberg-Richter maybe a Russian submarine exploded in the ocean. Then it stopped. Silence. A blue light had fallen along the distant mountains. He finished . . . whatever he was doing then went to sleep.

Jim is a very tall man he stooped in the kitchen in fact he had to bend slightly in all the rooms of the house eight feet eleven point one inches tall and four hundred and ninety one pounds heavy. His wife Deborah sat on a stool at the table. A baby highchair. She was twenty-two point three inches tall and her weight at that time was nine pounds. She was thirty-five. He was twenty-nine. She used a ladder at the sink to wash dishes. Their children, three of them, were all about the size of most of their enemies and neighbors: a hundred fifty pounds five feet eight inches.

Let's fox-trot in the moonlight do a dance to the lights from the apartments a screen of eyes on a flat midnight face.

Leo who follows the mules steps across broken barbed wire into a pasture he crosses a creek a dry rib and a river bed then he sleeps in the hollow of a log while the mules stand and fan flies. Jim envies Leo.

Let's move in a circle to the music of old men half asleep on their guitars and horns. Jim takes Roslyn's hands and starts to dance.

Together Leo and Jim feed the mules and sleep with them.

Let's boogie all day to the radio up loud till the season the spell releases us to ourselves till the floor stands still. I can't get Al to join us.

They have crossed the threshold of the barn seven thousand times in the last three years. I throw my whole body into the moment. They are the Ingrams.

Do the bunny hop do the cakewalk do the twist. Julie has a natural ability.

Nicholas Zieff, drunk throwing up on himself. He walks along with his bottle in his left hand a bruise on his left cheek his suit is expensive so is his derby a painted lady is trying to pick him up and is arrested for indecent exposure.

We are flying above the clouds eating hot toast and butter and sipping bitter coffee. The doors and windows are airtight. My characters and I are real swift.

Why was he so far away, why had he rejected her, turned his back? Across the hall there was a pregnant woman screaming at her husband over the sound of the TV.

Abruptly Ros is in the elevator going down.

Down.

She doesn't know where she's been. But now she is definitely going down, and fast. Way down. The walls slide up. There is no way back. *Why had he gone?*

If only she could stop

or start. Her mouth is dry

"Right now a drunk woman sits at a drunk table with two drunk men," I say, "A fly is crawling into the woman . . ."

and she crosses herself. Why had he rejected her? Ah, it doesn't matter. Not now. Never did. She remembered

"The only way to get out of this show is to keep going all the way to the exit . . ."

how he felt, *in* her. Ahhhhhh.

And the pills; and the pain in the middle of her back. And the creep across the hall, somebody's husband, a daddy, always trying to make her.

It won't stop now. Ros? What does my name mean? Feels like morning sickness. Once the downward motion starts nothing can stop it. It won't stop. Scream, it won't help. The elevator plunges on tward the earth. Nothing will stop it now. *Oh, Jim oh Jim!*

Way down

"Blackness," I say, "hugs her till she releases the image of herself. Sends it to be developed."

at the bottom. Getting stiff; the hands begin to stretch; the arms; the fingers; the eyes. She pulls

"I cut into the nerve bed," Jim once said See?
herself. There is no end. She threw herself a thousand
years ago into the well and poisoned the water. She became
a detective in London and solved murder cases. The
generations at that time were deranged. The TV sets all
break trying to deal fairly with such information.

"She stumbles at the threshold of her life."

She is falling through "a tight sweet little hole" back to
the meaning of . . . everything. Even when we stop

"The elevator is hard and rough in its outer skin."

to sleep she continues to fall. Go on, lady!

The hall and the elevator are now on exhibition in the
worn area of the deep memory.

On the east side of the threshold the eye, the private
eye, continues to search for the proper light for the
landscape.

Her memory. How he came early one morning telling
her that it was all over. He left leaving a light showing
through the keyhole, for days. She went about crying and
finally her ears got stuck to the kitchen cabinets. Her
breasts fell off. Her hair fell out. Her teeth broke off,
falling back into her throat.

But that last fall: the plunging elevator containing her
last evidence, wrapped in a torn nightgown, reaches out to
the history maker and says

"You heard about the woman who died instantly upon
looking in the mirror while wearing her wedding gown."

excite me, excite me, thrill me, oh, thrill me till I come
. . . back for more!

1. Ros can we make it.

2. If you have to ask me that I'm worried.

3. Don't worry I know we can make it. It's just that there are so many other factors involved.

4. Race?

5. No not race my kids my work my career my public image so much.

6. I don't understand how any of those things are problems. I love you Jim and I need you and want a life with you.

7. I know I know. I want a life with you too.

8. What kind of life do you want with me Jim do I satisfy you sexually.

9. No question about it you do you know you do.

10. You satisfy me you're the first man in years who satisfies me. I've been so miserable I'd almost given up on men until we started giving each other a chance and I think it's good we didn't jump right into bed at the beginning. We were friends for a long time I like that it's the way it should be.

11. Yeah.

12. Julie hates me I hope she gets over that I want a good relation with your kids.

13. Yeah. Yeah I guess so. It's hard to figure her and that thug from Harlem she hangs out with. I don't know what she's trying to prove. He's clearly her inferior.

14. It's probably just a stage she has to go through she'll come out of it and before you know it she'll marry some nice middle class boy from Harvard or Yale you'll see.

15. Yeah.

16. What's going on with Deborah these days.

17. Deborah is beginning to find a new life for herself I think she'll be all right I suspect she's seeing somebody already. It's all very sad.

18. Why is it sad.

19. Because life is so fucking sad so goddamn fucking sad every way you look at it it's sad, sad *sad.*

20. I wouldn't say that Jim look we have each other and there's the future. The future isn't necessarily sad it's just that right now things are rough for you but you're handling it all very well. I just wish you'd pull yourself through it a little faster you know the longer you let it drag out the more painful it's going to be for all concerned.

21. I know. Yeah I know. You're right. I wanted to make the break gently but I guess that's not possible I guess it will have to be ugly and painful.

22. Sure it will. Just do it. Life is too short to fuck around with indecision. Just do it. Your kids won't ever turn against you they love you.

23. You think so?

They are headed back to Duck Pond. At a corner near where the VW is parked Julie waits for Al to assist a blind Black man across the street. Half way across the blind man says to Al, I sure do thank you son I sure do you know I tried to get one of my own peoples to help me a little while ago but they ain't no good keep right on walking like nobody's business.

The hot sunlight is pouring down on them as they speed back. Julie at the wheel. Eighty in a fifty-five mile zone. Julie's talking about Sara: You see, as long as I'm unhappy and frustrated and in need of her advice she advises me and our relationship then and only then works fine everything is peaches and cream but just let things start going well for me like now and she gets very bitchy I don't know I think it's jealousy what'd you think of her, Al I mean really think of her be honest with me.

Holding the steering wheel with one hand she reaches over and unzips him and takes it out. I need to touch you she says like this.

Sara said you seemed remote unfriendly like. *Melodrama sentimentality irony.* In the past Sara has always felt at liberty to pass judgment on the people I've been involved with mainly I guess because before now I wasn't seriously involved with anybody except Johnny Hawkins you know the musician I told you about I mean she always had something negative to say about the people I brought around. I don't know I think Sara's and my friendship is just about over and that in a way makes me pretty sad. She

166

said I should be careful and cautious about my relationship
with you she reminded me of the times in the past when
I've been hurt all my traumas but how can you have a
satisfying love relationship and at the same time be
cautious if there's no trust what's the point.

They shot by a crowded scene of a violent accident.
State troopers standing around three cars that had
rammed into each other. *Atmosphere.*

About fifty naked men locked into their personal habits are riding fat brown pig-like creatures, shooting arrows at smaller pig-like creatures running for cover, the bushes or holes in the earth where they hide deep in warmth and darkness for years before they are transformed, reborn, and come out so different nobody knows they are the same creatures.

The group of young men including Oscar and Patrick who went into that sea shell stayed a long time. Rumor has it they are revolutionaries being watched by the children including Cynthia Neal in first grade.

Wounded Oscar sleeps in an unpainted barn listening to the promise his father made thousands of years before the world started.

"Great Savings Through Superior Pussy." Now I was the only one among us who sternly opposed that pitch the factory the warehouse the main office were in uproar. Trudy designed the catalogue of artificial vaginas and she suggested another approach . . .

We sell directly. Direct distribution method results in our remarkably low prices. The ones with hair on them and the real smell and warmth we have sold to kings and queens and princes and princesses and congressmen and dictators and . . . Branches in . . .

Observe also no minimum order is required from persons who purchase their pussies in person we also carry a complete line of penises but that is not my department . . .

We can assure you we are working for the spaceage the United States of America and its Territories sincerely yours Superior Pussy, Inc. Manufacturers and Distributors Inlet, Connecticut. Very spiritual huh?

Some people say that the *things* are eating them. It's really the trees they eat people at night vampires come out and dance on the graves of Inleters who died before their time. Dogs start meowing and the pussies start barking.

I've seen those who walk around late nights with huge human heads attached to the bodies of lizards and snails bats and crows some say we need an exorcism here the straight citizens are scared.

I watched from the window the action was really getting heavy.

For years various strangers have called me at four in the morning asking if I'd fix it for them when I say fix what they hang up.

African Print Thresholds Sexy Thresholds Acrylic Thresholds Iron Thresholds Rosewood Thresholds Oak Thresholds Satin Trimmed Thresholds Velvet-Lined Thresholds Cozy Thresholds Light-Weight Thresholds Gold-Plated Thresholds. All-Season Thresholds!

"I want you to get out of town before sundown." Already I stood at the edge.

The narrow street was filthy and bleak Jim Ingram stood there in his bright suit unable to see through his rimless glasses. When the boys thought it was clear that they'd shot out his eyes they ran. They did not know he was fighting for their rights.

Cozy Washable Thresholds Padded Thresholds Heavenly Hill Thresholds Last Judgment Thresholds Country Thresholds Exotic Thresholds French Styled Thresholds Snowy White Thresholds Magical Thresholds. Sale Ends Without Prior Notice.

Oscar and Patrick went down to the creek set their poles and took a nap.

The cobblestones beneath Jim's feet feel slick from years of slime.

Trying to get out of town Al ran across a vacant lot and fell into a pile of garbage.

They were alone together at Duck Pond for a change. Al said I've been thinking I don't think we have as much in common as we should have for things to really work right. I mean background for instance. You come from a middle class way of life and well you know where I come from beans and rice and if we were lucky a little fat back or neck-bones. All your life it's been vacations in Europe and good schools and Africa and steaks and an open fire on a cold night. I mean we're worlds apart and when I say this I'm not happy about it because Julie I want us to make it together. But we should be able to talk about our differences. And take your friends they may not be the kind of people I can get along with. And I wouldn't even want to take you around some of my friends because they ain't always on their best behavior. Some of them be out there doing anything just trying to stay alive and at times they even look weird to me. The only time they have big tender steaks is when they buy it from the dude on the street who's just ripped off the meat market.

Julie's smile is bitter. I've never heard you talk this way before is this the real Allen Morris finally revealing himself.

Al did not answer.

Listen I've lived among poor people in Europe *and* Africa and I've shared my things with others who've had less. I remember riding on a train through the south of France once and I gave my lunch to the children in the compartment with me.

Al started laughing and couldn't stop for a long time. He finally wiped away his tears.

Julie is reading the newspaper to Deborah: "A special

State Senate Emergency Investigation Committee has been appointed by the governor to look into the possible threshold misconduct of a group calling itself The Isrealites. . ."

Deborah laughs. In jest she says, "We *is* real light."

"What?"

"An old joke. Uppity colored people."

"Mom," says Julie, "this is *serious!* This is no time to joke. This threshold law is —"

"At our doorstep."

"*Mom!* Cut it out!"

"Sorry, dear."

Deborah leaves the deck chair and places her arm around Julie who is leaning against the railing holding the newspaper.

(Telegram)

THE FAITH OF THE MUSHROOM WAS DISMANTLED AND THE PENIS PEOPLE REVOLTED EARLY IN HUMAN HISTORY STOP THE UPHEAVAL STEMMED FROM THEIR FAITH IN KENNETH PATCHENS GREEN DEER AND THEIR FRENZY WAS CAUSED BY INDULGENCE IN SECRETS AND GOD KNOWS WHAT ELSE STOP MYTH AND GEOMETRY POWER MALENESS AND FORCES BEYOND THEIR CONTROL STOP TO A LARGE EXTENT THE SECRETS OF THEIR RITUALS AND CULTISM WERE CAREFULLY CONCEALED IN THE BODIES OF THEIR SLAUGHTERED HEROES STOP RELIGIOUS HISTORIANS HAVE DISCOVERED THE DEAD SEX WHICH REVEALS THE FUNCTION OF THE SACRED THRESHOLD WHICH ALSO HAS A SECRET NAME NOT YET UNDERSTOOD BY RESEARCHERS OF THE LINK BETWEEN GREEK LATIN AND OTHER INDO-EUROPEAN LANGUAGES STOP SECRECY PROVIDED THE PENIS PEOPLE WITH IMMUNITY FROM THE ANTI-SEXUAL PEOPLE WHO CONTROLLED THE DOORWAY TO THE UNQUESTIONABLE STOP KNOWLEDGE OF THEIR FERTILITY DIETY LEAKED ANYWAY ONCE IT WAS DISCOVERED GENERALLY THAT ALL THE GODS WERE PRETTY HARD TO SEPARATE STOP

"What possible use would a green deer be to anyone?"

—Kenneth Patchen
Memoirs of a Shy Pornographer

THE INLET TENNIS COURTS
(Saturday)

Court 1	Court 2	Court 3	
Rose Marie	*Deborah*	*Al*	
WHACK	WOK	WACK	WACK
WHOCK	WAK	WOCK	WOCK
WHACK	WOK	WACK	WACK
	WAK		
WHACK	WOK	WA	CK
	WAK		
WHACK	WOK	WO	CK
WHOCK	WAK		
WHACK	WOK	WACK	WOCK
	WAK	WOCK	WACK
WHACK	WAK		
WHOCK	WA	WO CK OCK	
	WOK		
	WAK	WA CK OCK	
Julie	*Jim*	*Barbara*	

174

THE INLET PUBLIC LIBRARY

Books (a sampling):

A History of Traffic Violations in Inlet, Connecticut. V. E. Smith. 1972.

Recent Progress in the Study of Disorders of the Colon and Rectum. S. Drobni and M. Feher. 1972.

Reconstructive Surgery of the Brain Arteries. F. T. Merei. No date.

101 Unexplained Events of the Recent Past Including the Re-election of the Mayor of Inlet. V. E. Smith. 1973.

The Physiology of Violin Playing. O. Szende and M. Nemessuri. 1971.

Understanding the Religious Significance of Class. H. J. Pope. 1965.

Ego-Psychological Implications of the Threshold Law. J. Van Love. 1976.

The Death and Birth of God. D. M. Denn. 1969.

Werewolves Who Marry Christian Women. H. K. Hirzel-Grúz. 1966. English-German.

A Psycho-Analytical Interpretation of the Novel "Emergency Exit" by Clarence Major. John S. Narcissism. 1979.

Power and Money on Heavenly Hill. R. E. W. Williams. 1969.

Voodoo Babies. H. K. Hirzel-Grúz. 1967. English-German.

Le Suicide, Etude de Sociologie. E. Durkheim. 1927.

How To Speak in Tongues and Be the Life of the Party. P. Greene. 1978.

Adventures in the Last Judgment. R. Boke. 1968. English-Spanish.

Biochemistry of the Brain Tumours. N. Wollenman. 1974.

A Radiometric Examination of the History of Puritan County, Connecticut, from Its Inception to the Present Day. T. Zilboorg. 1979.

Close Inspection of the Vagina. D. D. Woolf. 1946.

A History of Sin. S. R. Porterfield. 1930.

The Black Middle Class in Puritan County: 1823-1923, With an Introduction by Rev. Joost D. Sutton. W. Bonaparte. 1925.

Regeneration and Wound Healing. G. Szántó. 1964.

Close Inspection of the Penis. D. D. Woolf. 1946.

Walking Your Infant Across the Threshold. C. Cseh. 1980.

Fart Prevention. R. Hung. 1943.

How To Make Friends with Witches. F. Parfenov. 1975.
The Threshold in an Age of Television. R. Edwards. 1981.
Thresholds: The Anthology of Poems of Local Inlet Poets on the New Law. Edited by D. Hale, Jr. No date.
101 Uses for Goose Grease. C. Lynch. 1931.
Women Respond to the Threshold Law. An Anthology. Edited by M. Stephens. 1976.
Men Respond to the Threshold Law. An Anthology. Edited by M. Stephens. 1976.
101 Ways to Skin a Guru. Humor. C. London. 1979.
Contributions to the Study of Luck, Bad and Good. A. Millbank. 1942.
Spiritualism and the Threshold. B. Alexander. 1988.
Inlet: A Tourist City. J. A. Williams. 1960.
A Handbook of Clean Living. R. Mancini. 1961.
The Power Structure of Inlet. G. Putnam. 1966.
An Outline of Prostitution at Inlet. T. Lyon. 1974.
Murder Cults at Inlet: How To Abolish Them. S. Otto. 1972.
Night Life at Inlet: How To Abolish It. S. Otto. 1973.
Rock Music and Inlet Youth: Five Stages of Containment. H. Wain, A. Weaver, and P. Marlow. 1970.
On Spells. W. Kenworth, Jr. and Y. MacDonald. 1919.
Dissection of the Brain. R. Kós. 1966. Russian.

Films (a sampling):

A Word on the Previous Chapter. Director: A Late Consumptive Usher to a Grammar School. 1979.
Brother Shandy. Director: Dr. Slop. 1979.
Penis People vs. the Anti-Sexual People. Director: Bob Roberts. 1979.
Black Humor. Director: Dr. Feinstein. 1979.
Vic Has Janice's Key. Director: Miles Smartas. 1979.

Tapes (a sampling):

Why Not Use the Shifting Method of NO? Narrator: Jerry K. Smith. 1979.
Why Not Throw in a Poem or Two? Narrator: Jonathan B. Zolar. 1979.

Julie went in the house to make supper she was brooding. Her movements were slow and stiff.

Al went down the path to the lake. He felt like just about anybody and himself but he was not even a Hemingway character though he was about to go out alone on the lake in a boat like a Hemingway character. He was ready for some action. A crawling plant moved along the ground at his feet. It said good morning.

Al sat on a large rock near the edge of the water. He picked up a handful of tiny rocks and pitched them one at a time into the lake watching the splashes. Poot came down and sniffed around for a moment then disappeared. For a long while there was no one in sight; just the lake its afternoon color and its fresh smell, the burnt garbage in the clearing behind him causing a sting in his nose. Now and then a ripple on the flat lake. Then the bluntness of a motorboat's motor.

But where was the boat? Who was the boatman? Certainly not Papa LaBas.

There is mystery in these here back woods. Then he saw the boat, in far too close for a motorboat. Could it be. Al moved back into the shade of the path. One person. A man. It *is* the same boat: red white and blue.

Be sure now man yeah I'm sure all right he's yours get ready you ain't got nothing but your bare hands so work fast then there's still the chance that within minutes you can be a dead duck, a dude with a bullet in his head.

The man has the rifle standing up in the empty seat beside him. Is he the one are you sure you sure.

Al leaped up onto the rock in one solid motion and almost in the same motion jumped from the rock into the boat when it was close enough. The character in the boat, a young white man who is startled and who reaches for his rifle, loses control of the boat. Al kicked the rifle into the water.

"Nigger," the man murmurs as though to himself, like someone who is mixing the ingredients for a cake might say, "Eggs," when arriving at the point when eggs are necessary.

As Al struggled with the man he realized that he was not the one who had shot at him that day in Little Duck Pond. He was not even the one who had been with the one who shot at him. This realization took away some of his anger and drive.

The white man turned red. He pushed Al into the water then jumped in after him, located the rifle, then started beating Al over the head with it.

"Sonofabitch! What's the big idea!"

Al could not answer. He was sitting in the water up to his neck. Al was dazed.

The young man staggered back, out of breath, and rested against the side of his boat. The motor was still puttering. Buzzing bumping stuttering.

The young man spoke again. "What's the big idea?" The place where the rifle had struck Al's head was now swollen.

A few walking plants came down to the edge to see what all the fuss was about. Poot arrived too. The dog barked and barked until Julie arrived.

Some children from a nearby house were watching at a safe distance. They were standing ankle-deep in the water forty yards away.

Julie said to the young white man, "It's probably true that you drink sloe gin and use Synthetic Blood and own a Rib Joint and know the whole scene of The Night Club and The Open Door and invest in the Gateway of Life and that your parents own Absolute Thresholds and that you are a member of the Scottish Presbyterian Church that you attend the yearly conference of Emergencies and that you had a bit part in The Punishment of the Uncircumcised that you buy your fuck films at the Glans Removal that your grandaddy runs City Hall that your mama screws photos of Tom Mix that your brother is a community organizer in a Black section of Inlet that you believe in dim lights and card tables that you eat at Nick Tamucci's, but tell me Joe Smith, my dear friend and neighbor, where do you really get on . . ."

"Hell, Julie, he jumped me first! Jumped out of nowhere and tried to kill me."

Julie looked at Al.

Al spoke. "The names all run together. I can't sleep any more. I keep getting ideas. Sandy Janice Gayl John Charles Pete Joe Roy Eddie. The monks. The giant birds. John Keats and Cervantes. Oscar Wilde. I don't know any of these people yet they keep popping into my head All I want is some bread and a nice high, loose shoes and tight pussy. I swear I don't want to give anybody no trouble. Cindy Charles Hal Stella Barry Sara Rosetta Roslyn Patrick Alla Blake. Listen I don't want to get into their business. I just want to mind my own. I just want to stay nice and high and cool and not have to fight the crooks who run this place. It drives me insane to go downtown and see how white the world is. I want to build a tunnel and walk through it till the end."

"See," Julie said to the white man, "he's innocent."

Message from Up Above

THERE IS NO SUCH THING AS AN EMERGENCY
THERE IS NO SUCH THING AS AN EMERGENCY
THERE IS NO SUCH THING AS AN EMERGENCY
THERE IS NO SUCH THING AS AN EMERGENCY

Message from Down Below

"I are illone . . . jetz me . . ."

—George Herriman
Krazy Kat

They shaved the hair from Deborah's vagina. Her legs apart the live thing came out. "Push mother." Jim was nervous waiting. His eyes were hot he wanted a son. But the city was surrounded by wild animals. *This city is still surrounded by something dangerous!* The infant girl crying. Mother, long straight hair in a single black braid down her slender back a gold crown around her head sparkling. Pink gown. Orange juice, white walls. Troops going by. Thud. Machine gun fire and broken jewelry shops. Jim stands just inside the waiting room waiting. Dark green double breasted suit. Dark blue glasses. Slicked-down thin hair one hand in pocket. A thick cigar juts from his thin lips. Big thick head. "I could use a double shot of gin." He watches the soft hair in his wife's armpits as she takes her hair loose. She's now combing it affectionately. The nurse enters smiles. How's mother today. Her eyes are made up. They sparkle. Her white stockings are pulled tightly around Jim's muscles where his imagination is bloated with puss.

Two strong truck drivers live together they sleep together when they are in town at the same time.

They take turns. One steps forth into the blue light. Two sees that nothing happens. Nobody claps. One's face is purple. Two's hands are orange. The light behind him is orange. He has no face no fingers no strings on his shoes no belt no arms no body no hair. One has hair the color of red mud what else can happen. One and two drive each other crazy.

One foot slides outside the acceptable area.

Jim is caught through the stomach by the blade of a giant knife. He is busy painting his self portrait. The face is not his. Perhaps the painter is deranged. Below on the street the celebration goes on. Bulls are being chased through the streets. One splits a door and enters a living room where a family is eating supper. Piles of mulch enrich the air.

The trees are rusty the road is red the drawbridge has turned black. You're standing in the doorway watching the sky turn dark. It's going to rain. On the hill above your house a man is nailed to the cross. Buzzards circle his head.

Barry Sands sits on the top step against the door. He's strumming a gypsy guitar singing a Spanish love song a great oh so awful whine in his voice an ancient sound. A dog appears behind him standing half way in and half way out of the house. He licks Barry's elbow. Barry's fingers gently pluck the strings his red shirt is open at the collar his watch has the correct time his parents are wealthy. He plans to enter law school next year he plans to penetrate the business world five years from now.

"Three in the morning, I left my yellow car in a black parking lot. At five thirty the sun struck it. It glowed for ten minutes: a giant grapefruit full of glitter and rainwater. While inside, I imagine, The Beatles were singing *Here Comes the Sun*. I had only to open the door to allow the music to spread."

Elmar Blake is caught in a mob of elbows and faces. His legs turned watery he knew he was going to die. He *knew* it. Pushing shoving pinching biting scratching screaming. A baby held high above the heads, desperately. He stumbles and falls to his knees. He closes his eyes and curls up with his arms over his head. Like this at the center of the mob he suddenly feels safe. He begins to sing a song he sang as a child. Were they storming the same palace they had stormed for thousands of years or at the steps of the Pentagon. When he hears the huge doors fall he knows the emperior will soon follow. So exciting is this thought it causes him to bite the inner skin of his arm till the taste of blood reaches his tongue.

Roslyn is drunk. You know Roslyn. She's lost, singing one two, buckle my shoe, three four, close the door. She's dreaming up bad names to call Jim. He promised to call hours ago. One two, five six, pick up . . .

She kisses the image of herself in the bathroom mirror then smears lipstick across it. She stands back and looks at it suspiciously. Make up something.

"Speak softly," says Nicholas Zieff, "and carry a big stick." He opens the door to the toilet and goes in. Roslyn is there, smiling.

We haven't had any flashbacks have we how can we have a decent American novel without at least one good flashback? I'm not bringing this in arbitrarily. This is truly the proper time. But to whom to flashback is the question. How about—? You guessed it!

In Inlet each year there is a contest to see which teenage girl can smile the brightest smile. Say cheese. The all-American light complexioned Black girl. Hello Black girl Julie. Sloppy bright shirt and dungarees of stiff blue stuff. Tight tension in the eyes. Hello eyes smile eyes say something cute. Be serious win a scholarship prove they're all wrong become a . . . ah doctor! not a cheerleader a babysitter! not a nurse for Dr. Queen. I, the author, sent on the whip-cream to match her Black American smile. She stands in the Magic Doorway waving to her friends of Inlet High. Hi high! Hi ho.

Patricia, hi, Patricia. Hi Julie. Hi hi Barbara.

Hi.

Hello.

That's the beginning and here she is in one of the seven sisters. Hi sisters. This is my country too. Hi girls. Strange old facts. Can you remember when pleasure was greater than pain? How do you do pain?

Some characters are trapped in this erotic fantasy and do not want to escape they are secure in the pain of it and the pleasure can never match the pain. Do you want to escape?

I simply water the plants here. Other people who believe in abnormal blue grass weed the flowers *and* the grass. This is my front: behind it all I manipulate the characters and pretend I have nothing to do with the *real* people. Between me and you I control them too.

The Black girl adores Robert Walker in old movies she also adores Marcello Mastroianni in new movies. She's conscious of the wet spot in the dead center of her under-pants. Damp vanilla. I touch it taste it come out of it return to it. I am that I am she is that she is.

Patricia and Rose Marie are my best friends. We dress alike wear our hair alike. Hello alikeness.

Is it fun to be Jezebel in the dark? The boys force Pat into positions she cannot resist. She *says* she doesn't like it but being a blonde what can she do. Trade in her blue eyes?

Gordon is just another name. Hello Gordon welcome to the fiction. We know you're trying to make Pat. It won't be difficult. Ask the fellas.

Rose Marie and I sleep late on Saturday but Pat is up early washing her Great American Hair. Hello blond hair, welcome to American Mythology 101. Or is it 501? Grad School.

My name is Sue. This is not the kind of story I'd write for Creative Writing 6.6V. Vestal cunt at the center of a moral struggle would be more interesting to an American audience. I wear Puritan prescription glasses. One day contact me when I'm on the silver screen saying I told ya so. Excuse me Patty is coming.

Sue you're light enough to wear blue frost eyeshadow and crushed coral lips. Where is your secret wink, you sneaky betrayer.

Gordon says, Ah do you like the gristle call me what you will.

Yes yes, Gordy, but I'm no doxy no hellcat no virgin either I'm no madonna no libber, I'm simply me. Excuse me, Barbara. Gordon this is Barbara. That girl standing in the doorway over there is her sister Julie.

Say gang let's go down to the corner cafe for a coke what ya say. You coming Gordy?

Leave him alone all he wants is leg he's crude one part of him floats about thirty yards above his head and he's never made contact with it and it's the most important part.

Gordon smiles a bitter evil smile. Say cheese girls. They all give him the Great American Cheese smile.

Roslyn is still drunk. She's trying to make up her bed in the dark. "Speak gently and carry a weapon."

Jim kisses her while she sleeps lovely Ros.

Give me titles pick a number. Any number. Pick a word any word.

"It is natural to suppose that a rose is a rose is a rose. It is as natural to suppose that everything is why they went."

—Gertrude Stein,
How to Write

Rosyln: Julie, I wish you'd try to understand how I feel about your father. Would you like a cup of sea I mean tea?
Julie: No, fwqaz fghksadrt. You've fuyrtyui and he's hwqazpo. I'm sorry you've fdswqpol. It's too bad.
Roslyn: I wish fgrepolnb. But I guess hgrtyolnmhj, jhgk.
Julie: Body language tells a lot. Fdepojkhas. Fghret. Uh?
Roslyn: Well, in our post-industrial society what can we expect? It's not easy. You sure you wouldn't like a cup of tea and a pacifist anti-novel to look at?

Alla Blake can almost nurse it feeling its huge mouth its unexpected teeth chewing viciously on her raw thick red nipple.

Again she was on her knees washing the blood from the garment she hid last night. Behind her the bathroom door was locked.

"The individual is nowhere in sight." I looked toward the crowd.

Way in the back of Alla was a group of businessmen all wearing the same necktie. They were locked in their offices. Eyes. Their eyes were orange slits in black holes like the Ku Klux Klan.

The other nipple is also sore and damaged.

It began to rain. Hourari got up and turned off the two lamps, opened the curtain, which looked out onto the clutter of roofs, walls, buildings, all now drenched in a heavy cosmological blue darkness with indifferent lights jumping in it. Finally, he lay down on the bed and pulled his coat over his legs, shivering. Outside, a crouched running form, a person, male, moved across the cityscape, the skyline. A terrified rat seeking shelter. He jumped from one roof to another and kept on. A gun in his hand, moving. Meanwhile, a light from the sky struck the runner and moved away, turning him for that moment into a glowing flame.

Hourari is now telling Julie about it: While deep sea diving I found a ship. It contained a floating gin palace, a man sleeping with his raincoat over his legs, a killer escaping from the scene of the crime, kids jumping rope on a roof top, a synthetic blood company, a man up a flagpole, wolves hanging around an open doorway, a threshold stained with blood. His girl said: Sure, you told me about it already.

I was with Jim again in his bedroom in a rooming house in the south. I was near the door, Jim at the window. Jim does not plan to sell thresholds only black holes.

Rea said, "I shouldn't let you touch me you've been with that whore. I hate you for that."

If the night is cold hard and surrounds us with blue muddy rain, take me by the hand. So strong has been my thrust that at the moment when a single tear leaves me, expressing my fear, suspecting not so much that I am now ready to die, but that I am losing yet another large space in myself. That space may be half the time I've lived. It is hard to drive through New Jersey with a beard and long hair. Hold me close.

. . . I've spent two weeks in bed with people lifting me from it only briefly to change the sheets. They also came to draw blood from my arms. This is done with needles. My three windows show the . . . what is it? Each day the sky is different: cold wet bright dry clear blue. And so on. Someone sent flowers. A woman I love sits here in the room knitting. She comes in the afternoon and leaves at early evening. Soft-spoken men in white jackets stop by to see how I feel. I sleep lightly. The room can be made cold or hot. I keep it cool. In the beginning, they attached a cord to my left arm and through it, fed fluids into me. I closed my eyes and saw what was going to happen inside me. It is happening now:

The logs are piled against the dam. All the parts, the flesh and the stone, connect. When the word reaches the eye, it opens the brain, a crater, it triggers the landscape— complete with sunset, sunrise, moon, storms and seasonal change—whether or not the great dark, dark space inside responds to the proper signals.

The African in search of the mysterious substance called Black Humor wandered into the Kansas House of Representatives recently installed in the Inlet Museum complete with live, shotgun-toting figures in top hats. The African was so stunned by the sight of so many dangerous-looking white men that he forgot about Black Humor and blurted out: Has anybody seen my gal? Rather than laughing at the African's gimmick they all shot at him but like the trickster rabbit taught in Black Literature classes the African managed to escape unharmed. Long live the African!

Al takes Julie's hand. Let's go for a walk. So they go down and sit on the big rock near the water.

Al is not at ease: what if the white man with the rifle returns. He picked up a handful of tiny rocks and started pitching them into the lake making ripples. Julie watched the ripples too.

She took a deep breath and smelled the damp dense trees. A dog barked a few times. Where was Poot?

Giving Al a sharp and painful look Julie said, It's awfully hard for me to talk to him.

Who?

My father. If only I could *talk* to him I think so much could be resolved but he won't listen to me he refuses it's just a lack of courage on his part you see Al he's afraid to expose his deepest thoughts to me.

Al thinking: why should he.

He should *expose* himself to me but he's afraid of me I can feel it he doesn't want me to get too close to him even the few times we've danced together he was uneasy.

Why do you want him I mean *what* do you want from him?

Al I should think it's obvious I want my father to love me I'm his daughter he's never been able to love any of us and now he's running off to . . .

Julie started crying. Like a character in a soap opera she wiped away her tears and blew her nose.

Al threw a rock out as far as he could and watched it splash. The ripples were large and blue with the white of clouds in them.

Poot came up along the edge of the water sniffing at the wet sand.

A snake danced in the sky above the ripples. There was nothing unusual about its movements.

Julie suddenly turned to Al. Do I bore you when I talk about mom and dad?

His kindness took command. He said, No.

It's just that the whole situation leaves us all so I don't know dad has convinced himself that he can't confide in any of us not mom not even Barbara his favorite and certainly not Oscar he hardly knows Oscar his own son the only impression Oscar has of dad is this bigtime civil rights guy who gets his name in the newspapers it's really terrible I hate to think what Oscar's life is going to be like later on but dad feels now that the only true friend and real support he has is in that homewrecking white woman he's head-over-heels in love with.

She clamped her lips together and for a moment she was breathing furiously through her nose with her dark eyes closed.

Al threw another rock out. He felt like a character in a movie. Hello movie character.

It's awful, Julie said, and it's really illogical because we are the ones who've loved him the longest and the deepest. Tears were flowing down her cheeks. I mean how can he be so sure of her after all they haven't been intimate until recently and did I tell you she actually seduced him as the result of a bet she made it was a game—a game she was playing with one of the other employees in my father's office she had this bet with a guy she used to go with see and she said to this guy he told us all about it later that she could make even an old stuffed shirt like James Russell Ingram that's what she actually called him an old stuffed shirt and that's how it started she *is* very attractive and apparently always felt sure of herself so she phoned in sick one day and after work dad stopped by to see how she was doing and there she was in her sexy bed and with him in her bedroom she had him where she wanted him well you can imagine the rest and she won her bet.

Julie's sigh was filled with self-righteous disgust.

He's such a sucker oh god I hate to see him so completely
out of his mind can you imagine what it must be like for
mom to watch this happening to him I just don't know what
to think or feel any more but he's still my father and I want
him I want him to wake up before it's too late have you
noticed how distressed he is he's really falling to pieces he
claims he hasn't made any final decision but I suspect the
final one is pretty obvious anyway I sincerely doubt if he
can see what a slut this woman Roslyn Carter is I told you
about her her history I just can't understand how he can
just up and wrench himself from everything in his life just
completely overturn all the years of love and devotion and
goodness and warmth a whole life he has shared with one
of the finest most lovable women in the whole wide world
and for a trampy white woman it frightens me Al and now
from what he tells us Roslyn is threatening to drop out
putting pressure on him says she can't go on living with his
indecision and on our side he feels guilty for the pain he's
causing mom and us so he's eating his heart out sometimes
I fear he'll crack up under the strain.

Al threw a rock way out.

And what's worse for dad is he probably feels that
Roslyn is deceiving or manipulating him he can't help but
suspect he's no different from all the past suckers in her life
she has this pattern of taking men from their wives then
abandoning them when she's won the game but my father
may be the biggest sucker of them all because he's planning
to marry her a woman with children I just hope he doesn't
make a premature decision I mean for his own sake I'd hate
to see him get hurt so deeply and if she really loves him how
can she exert so much pressure on him for a fast decision
anyway he has doubt and as long as he is in doubt there is
hope he'll come to his senses and realize . . .

Poot jumped into Julie's lap and she hugged the wet
dog as it licked her cheeks.

TV screen: face, voice: "At noon today city police attempted to arrest a woman who resisted arrest. The woman was stopped for questioning in connection with the violation of the threshold law. Her name is being temporarily withheld. . . ."

Julie says, "Shit!"

" . . . . "
" . . . . "
" . . . . "
" . . . . . "

You went up on the rock to see who was coming across the desert so fast on a golden pony. It was the devil wearing a white sheet. You turned back to your horse, Bill, who was drinking from the river. Hey Bill you said take a look at this mean motherfucker coming here. Bill only groaned and continued to drink. The horseman rode out of the sunlight into the shade as you watched. He passed from the shade into darkness as you still watched. Finally he crossed the border and entered another land.

All those who can walk or crawl or run reach out falling trying to get there, where the sun is going down late in the afternoon with its long streams of light coming down at a sixty-degree angle through the thick masses of pine and oak.

A hammock swings between two trees. Jim and Roslyn resting in it legs dangling facing each other eyes closed not sleeping. Inside the nearby house the doorbell rings telephone rings dog barks the children yell. Jim opens one eye Roslyn opens her mouth. Twitches. Wiggles one toe.

Julie and Sara Neal were found pissing on a diamond-studded threshold in City Hall. The woman police who arrested them said they did not resist arrest.

Old women in black selling lace, woven and knitted things. They sit patiently on low stools along the giant walls of government buildings. Their faces pink red. Hair iron gray. Hands thick knotted fingers. Tight mouths. Blank eyes. One with a large square straw basket balanced on her head moves urgently along the sidewalk toward the open door of the public toilet for women.

Old men here marry young women. They stand in the garden looking worried. The women are cute, well dressed (they wear evening gowns before noon) and the men wear turtleneck sweaters and jeans. They look younger than they are. The leaves sparkle in the rain water. The women have tiny breasts wear rings on all their fingers. They like to slide their fingers in and out of the rings.

Jim stood with his elbows on the brass. Bartender Kute smiled said sorry don't serve niggers here Jim said that's all right I never drink them. Give me a scotch and soda. Kute reached under the counter and brought out his Colt. It galloped down the bar and out the place into the dusty main road. Everybody in the joint fell out laughing said to the light complexioned black man where you from pal. Rudo said drinks on me set him up Kute. We all God's own.

The breather could be your wife's lover or your own lover from the past who is on the verge of suicide. The breather is the girl who you made love with one night in a small town who said will you come back and marry me when you get your divorce. Or the guy who repaired your car and got to look under your dress. The breather is your mother when your father dies. Your sister when her son is arrested for running over an old man. The breather in the telephone is your grandmother come back from the grave. It's your past, your future; yourself, phoning yourself: trying to explain what happened though you don't know.

We all pitch in to help you. You have more baggage than any of us. It is hot the dirt road is hot the train station is long and a long way yet. We're tired it's a shame, you remind me of a movie star, Hollywood type. White man with white hair. The train will stop briefly if we get there in time. We will climb on and settle back in seats and watch the landscape beyond the window. Half way there I notice that your load is the lightest of all. Hey what're you trying to pull?

Are you willing to die for your country? Jim's boss asked him. They were sitting in the boss's parked car on a side-street. It was raining hard. Jim watched the streaks on the windshield for a long time before he spoke. Then he said I'd rather have my country die for me, sir. Jim's boss chuckled. The killer might say that, the gimmick fella might say something like that, even the breather might say that but James Ingram . . . Ah come on man you're one of us true and blue to the core. Jim smiled. I'm not a particularly complicated character am I.

He was consumed by his racial identity. The Black Professor. He was Black. The only aspect of Inlet's history he cared about was that of the experience of its Black people. In college he did a study of The Negro Upper Class. He hadn't known that there was such a thing. In his last year of college he wrote an essay on Ooo-Bop-She-Bam and one on His Hi De Highness of Ho De Ho and one on milltown honkytonk and barrelhouse and gutbucket life.

He wouldn't eat out in Inlet's finest restaurants because he was convinced that nobody could cook collard greens and corn bread and black eyed peas and ham hocks the way he could. So he cooked for himself and ate at home.

Three days a week he taught at Inlet College. His courses were, Introduction to The Black Experience and a five-hundred level course called, The Sense of the Black Experience. His students thought he was a drag.

He introduced them to Drag Gibson. They still thought he was a drag. He introduced them to taped music by All The Currently Popular Black Rhythm and Blues Stars and they warmed up to him a little bit but essentially still thought he was a drag.

To get away from his troubles he spent evenings at home reading Black history books. He had a secret ambition. One day he would go beyond these works in the field of the Black Experience. He would write and publish the definitive work on the Black Experience, especially in Inlet, Connecticut. Perhaps Wesleyan University Press would publish it.

Meanwhile, he spoke only to Black people and for sure did not hang out with white faculty.

On weekends he went to Harlem, New York, and cut

the rug. He also got drunk a few times and got ripped off. On one such occasion he was left standing in an alley in his drawers. But he still loved his people and swore by them.

Weekends, weekends. He never saw any of the plays at the Inlet Playhouse because it was white owned and the Black Auction Block Playhouse almost never had anything going. He did not know that it was also white owned.

He made up his mind to boycott the campus magazine, the *Inlet Journal of Literary Criticism,* because they had never published anything by a Black writer.

The boycott was a success. The following issued carried an essay by Addison Giles, a Black Critic, on the Responsibility of the Black Writer to the Black Community in Time of War and Peace.

Barry Sands.
Janice Page.
"When?"
"Tomorrow."

Consider the possible propriety of the relationship. Now look at the possible pitfalls, immediate and distant. Janice looked at him.

"I shaved the hair from my vagina."

"You what?"

Vic has a key to her place. This can be a problem. She remembered saying to Vic: "Two strong truck drivers who live together in my building sleep together when they are in town at the same time. Neighbors talk. Have you ever slept with a man?"

Vic still has the key.

If she could write she'd write it like this: In my protective inner self I want to blunt the pain of human stammering. I'd reach out for the wildness of love that can ease up quietly on the self and jab its dull blade into the soft heart-meat, the underside of the flesh, the civil mentality, the self; to take a chance like this is worth everything! *To be naked and trembling in the doorway, exposed to everything!*

The man at the piano stopped playing. Today is tomorrow. The candlelight flickered.

"My inner walls of self are vague structures," says Janice Page. She pushes her brown hair back from her face. She gives him a flickering glance.

"Did you ever see anybody caught through the stomach by a blade or a giant knife?"

"Can't say that I have. Why are you changing the subject?" The piano player started again and she looked at him. "I've seen bulls chased through streets, and I've sat up suddenly at four in the morning and noticed an endless number of doors closing all around me."

The waiter came for their order. Barry finished his Black Cow.

"You possess a rich and sweet mystery," he told her. Then he gave the waiter the orders.

When the waiter had gone she said: "My trees are rusty, my drawbridge has turned black."

"But your road is bright yellow."

"Yes, my road." She finished her scotch and soda. "On it I am often caught in a mob of elbows and faces. But strange: when I'm thrown into the center of it, I feel safe. I sing. I dance. I feel gentle and compassionate."

A lighted ship was going by on the bay. It blew its horn. They watched it pass.

"Once, at three in the morning I left my car in a black parking lot. At five-thirty, the sun struck it and it glowed for ten minutes like a giant grapefruit."

"I want to know everything about you."

"What about you?"

He laughed and the candlelight flickered. The piano music, *Stardust,* swam around them.

"You look like a man who easily possesses the terrible and sensuous authoritative presence we all envy, like a windstorm and a disruptor of the sunrise on the flatlands of some unnamed planet. So far out are you—yet you're not the Ultimate Prince. Confronting you some immodest desires have set up indecent housekeeping in the attic of my being."

He smiled. "You should be a poet."

She wanted to tell him the truth. In her wildest dream she would do anything for this stranger. She wanted to share

something with him!
Vic?

He's talking, telling about himself. He sees her through her eyes going away.

She's gone far away across her own landscape. She's searching for a large rich family she once saw gathered in a meadow. In her search she discovers fancy horses prancing around in an open field but not the family with the Chippendale antiques.

"You're drifting," he said. He clicked his tongue against his teeth. He banged his spoon into the cup.

The waiter brought the salads.

"In a way I'm just another girl in the office. I bet you've been out with every one of us. I hope not."

"I'm a wild beast at the end of a gallop across a white earthquake frozen at the moment of explosion. Save me. I love you."

"Would you go down on your knees to me, beg?"

"I'd eat ice cream and pumpkin pie for you. I'd go fly a kite. Point the way!"

"We sound like two characters in—"

Barry Sands smirked. "Who shaved the hair from your vagina? Unmask yourself!"

Janice giggled. "The Doorway of Life is guarded by fathers and step-fathers in cardboard helmets. Be careful, they have knives and guns in their boots."

"I'm always careful. I broke from the church. I found the body. It was not dirty. I cried that day I was so happy."

"Do you have spirits in you?"

"I am possessed by fireworks, lady. Sailors strut around on my chest looking for naked girls tattooed there years ago when I was a blazing fool!"

"Are you serious about me or do you just want to fuck?"

He wasn't paying attention. Listen! It was intense and rich and at the same time bright and light. And for a moment it seemed it would not stop. The anxiety and energy behind it, beneath it, were constantly pushing upward.

"What?"

"Your laughter."

"But I giggled."

"You looked embarrassed and twisted your napkin and blankly watched the movement of your own fingers crawling along the surface of your cold glass and I wanted to take you into my arms and call you Henry James, oh, Henry James."

"You're making fun of me!"

"No, I'm trying to *show* you what this is about. I love you, I want to kiss your feet!"

The waiter brought the smoked salmon.

"Listen," she said, "do you know Vic?"

They are all crowded into a lighthouse trying to see the Sound through a tiny window. Are we in Mystic, Julie asks. Camille Dumas smirks. Roslyn jerks. Barbara says, No we're in Nairobi. I see the Sound, says Gail. Jim is in the darkest corner beating a dog to death. He is surprised when it does not wake. Music by Stan Kenton is coming up the stairway. Rea blows her breath on the glass then draws a picture of Dick on it. There are hundreds of unidentified characters here too. Most of them are depressed because they haven't yet had their coffee and it's early. Athos Porthos Aramis are walking about with their swords drawn. I look for d'Artagnan but apparently he's not playing the game.

I hear the wind blowing around inside my body. My nose is open my eyes are closed I continue to wake up every morning before daylight aware that something beyond my control in me is living with a life of its own. It is snowing everywhere.

Locked in prison she eats ham and spinach and writes crude letters to . . . What can a drug-ridden whore look forward to at twenty-one: coma constipation fatigue psychosis withdrawal brain damage delusions and panic. Like the rest of us she has all the answers. It is raining everywhere.

You remember the young woman who tried to crawl inside the sound of her own music when she played the violin. She was Deborah at eighteen.

On blank forms there are spaces to be filled in. How can we learn how to respond. People must be broken down by age and sex.

The bed squeaks you can't see each other but you feel the uneasiness it's so thick you can slice it. Roslyn tries to cut through it anyway.

José Patrick and Oscar are naked in the river laughing and splashing water on each other. Their bodies are matted with twigs and dirt.

Roslyn gets drunk in beer halls she lifts her dress and rubs her stuff against the edges of tables. Everybody knows she's a showoff. Just look at her!

Sara Neal with her daughter Cynthia is in the vacant lot in a yoga position again. Sara has no idea that Cynthia works for the government.

The city is possessed by machines. It's suppose to be a big secret.

Every time they discover the savior they kill him, this time with broken whisky bottles legs from broken chairs cracked flower pots, anything. He does not become the savior till he's dead. They push him back into the *idea* of himself. What if he releases the idea of himself. Then what.

I deliberately selected defective lumber each piece was wrong but they all fitted into each other without nails. I'm building this thing.

The dream says Roslyn jumps out the window and nobody ever understands why. She and Jim eat out they eat in, they sleep in they sleep out. When he's in her he cannot understand her. When she is outside herself she knows too much.

I drive the nail into the wood. I thought I wouldn't need nails.

Oscar cuts the strips of wood with the automatic blade the strips like white flesh without blood dust settling on the eyelids. The buzz stays with me even weeks later while I'm reaching deep into the earth where some animal has died.

I went with Oscar from the warehouse to the office, both places were cold. From the inside in the window boxes of nails metal strips catalogs hammers and wood glue for sale. It's cold. My plans are freezing.

After Christmas the super sale on thresholds: rose colored thresholds perky thresholds feminine thresholds snuggly thresholds creamy white blue berry blue strawberry rose thresholds ripe banana yellow and king size thresholds!

That family that bottled grease was arrested. Jim was the first to see the news.

"Those of you who have colds *must* go to the drugstore." Roslyn was shocked to come upon this sentence in the newspaper. "Are we living in a dictatorial town?"

My plumber uses coffee grounds to unstop sinks he was arrested for this. In court he entered a plea of guilty though it was noted that fifty percent of the time his technique worked. Deep down in that hole who knows . . .

People driving home in cars alone have absolute privacy. Jim Ingram appreciates this time alone.

They let Al out of prison and he slept for days in a

washroom beneath the sink where the smell of women was still strong.

The boy who lit three cigarettes from one match was struck dead by lightning. His remains are kept inside his mother's imagination where there is room for a whole civilization. Al keeps having this dream.

I went to see the guru. His eyes were weak but he could still sit still in his first and last judgments. The librarians with rubber breasts were there too.

The cigars old men smoke are going to be taken from them one of these days then the whole world will reach its turning point, the threshold will revolve. Mr. Gimmick will have his day. Barry's fantasy of Julie will be consummated. Jim will return to his previous (ambiguous?) glory in Nairobi. The breather, yes, even the breather will have his day. The researcher will find his answers and the frontiersman will rest from his endless search! Glory be!

Deborah, he thinks.

His head contains a private ache. In the need to be alone he was alone, suffering. His ringing was answered and his telephone was slender. Against the table his hand stood. Deborah old enough to be my mother. In his limbs were claws. Raw spirit. Above a whisper. "Hello."

"Are you busy?"

Yes he was interested. But Deborah like this? In my aloneness sadness. No one's been here for days. This apartment is a dark cave hidden in the middle of a busy city. Yes Deborah you too are one of the sad ones, come to me, follow me, I am the way give up your life—give it to me—so that you can find it.

Deborah had to tell him her name though it was always on his mind. She cleared her throat.

"Don't tell me, forgive me. I always hear things from a long memory. Jim is with Ros. He calls her Ros now."

He laughs at himself. "How are you?" I'm a shadow to her. What am I to myself.

"Good *now* good very good."

"Yes, stop in."

She came overnight with an overnight bag.

He held her as she held him, he kissed her stern brownpink cheek. She kissed the wrinkle in his black chin. He needed to shave. His eyes were red.

Like characters in French literature they did this several times in different ways, little pecking kisses, mathematically precise kisses, unemotional kisses. She squeezed his right hand. That touch of the motherly middle-aged woman. The bone was there beneath the flesh. She pronounced his name, again, after all this time. A sweet

African name. The bone was still there.

She pulled back from the movement of their fingers. In her eyes a sad brightness. He watched it change colors.

He could smell her where she was worn thin. He could smell her wool, the suit she wore. She was hair, clean-smelling hair, and skin and she spoke gently when she spoke. Her eyes were bright with life, as though they were always witness to the most shocking event in the world. Always.

Kissed.

"Wha da you say we do something, huh?"

"Like—?"

"Oh, I don't know," she said, "*you* suggest something."

"Want to see a movie?"

"Christ yes! I haven't seen a movie in ages! You have a newspaper—let's see what's playing."

They open the newspaper many famous American movies are playing at the same time, which makes life very frustrating. Here they are:

Dr. Jekyll and Mr. Hyde	*The African Queen*	*Ben Hur*
Andy Hardy's Double Life	*The Big Sleep*	*The Wild Ones*
Birdman of Alcatraz	*The Wizard of Oz*	*Wild Orchids*
Alice in Wonderland	*Only Angels Have Wings*	*Key Largo*
Superman	*Star Wars*	*Saturday Night Fever*

The titles alone conjure up so much excitement one has to take a pill to calm down!

Going out, just for kicks, he carried her across the threshold, laughing at himself. She also laughed at him.

Downstairs in the hallway she stroked his rough hair, delighted by its sculptured look and texture.

In the taxi Deborah talked about herself, said she was beginning to pull herself together, go out more, look up old friends. "I keep telling myself: just think survival, *survival!*"

He paid and they entered the darkness then the light and brightness of *The Wizard of Oz* with Judy Garland.

And Deborah begins to talk back to the players. Real characters in the theatre are annoyed.

Back in the candlelight sip of his apartment, once again the couch was a place where their warm bellies touched. The radio on and the blanket covered their legs. Soft rock music one number after another.

She was again talking about her family. The husband who left her—or who was about to leave her.

"I feel no ill feelings. She *is* pretty, younger than me. She's white. His secretary."

"Actually everything has a privacy of spirit."

"I don't understand the lines in my hands."

"Listen, I once read a book called *Reflex* in which the characters were constantly talking *at* each other but almost to each other and it gave me the strangest feeling."

"We're like that?"

"Yes, yes yes yes yes yes. Oh, yes."

"I only hope my kids can adjust to this . . . thing. I mean, living without him. The youngest, the boy, is confused by it all. The romantic notion he's had about his father—all gone now. And the youngest girl, his pet, I think she's been *hit* the hardest."

He said something she didn't understand.

"I don't understand," she said.

He agreed that there was no understanding. He suggested that understanding might not be the solution.

His sturdy strong hand finally reached her mound.

"We might not be friends anymore."

"Just love, huh?"

"That's the way it would be."

"But I am and will remain your friend."

Later: "I have someone I'm seeing anyway."

"Do you love him?"

"We understand each other. He's my age."

As he thought about what appeared to be her honesty

his mind turned toward the beginning of a right angle.

He carefully tucked the blanket around her and left her there on the couch.

In his bed he was on the edge of sleep fighting the shapeless fear of death.

He felt her motion move the bed as she moved in.

They were furious, passionate. A shuddering orgasm. Until they reached out desperately toward separate angles.

Later: unable to sleep she put cotton in her ears. City noise. Took a sleeping pill. Hard to get to sleep outside her own bed.

Spoon fashion.

He did not give in to his doubt. A cold, brutal consideration approached him: *Am I being used?* At the moment there was an unknown plot. The action was there but it was not his action. The orgasm he enjoyed in a strange, destructive way. It was like something taking place outside his body. She had worked hard for her own orgasm and got it so she now slept half well. It was four-thirty in the morning.

In the morning they could hardly look at each other. He made coffee, keeping his back to her.

She wanted him again but did not dare ask. She said it by the way she touched him. He gave his answer by the way he moved away.

Over coffee they tried to smile at each other till it was time. And soon it was time.

Inlet shopping centers are flat, maps of the city are flat.

Things are getting tense. Julie is screaming: Let me in let me in let me in let me in let me in let me in let me in let me in let me in let me in let me in let me in let me in let me in let me in let me in let me in let me in let me in.

Deborah cut her fingernails on Tuesday married Jim and tried to live happily ever after.

Rea cut her fingernails on Friday night she "died" instantly she was a virgin.

Every time I think of something to say I request television time this time I want all men to lift all women across all thresholds because a man's doorway is holy. "Listen, jack, you can't be serious. What's wrong with a woman using her own two feet?" It's not her feet that concerns me I'm more concerned with her doorway.

Oscar threw a rock and broke a bottle then ran to hide behind the lumber.

At the Home of the Deaf Workers things are more interesting than ballet dancers. They know how to open and close doors without banging them.

Deborah is stretched out on the bed naked. She keeps her stockings on because the doctor thinks it's sexy. She told me she's not entirely convinced he's crazy. He locks the nurse out when she's there. It causes huge creatures to gallop through his imagination. She wears her heels in bed too. Her breasts are large and her nipples are plump. Thighs thick and short with a dash of red pubic hair between them.

The killer locked a lot of people in the freezer and shot them through the head then he opened his own head to see if the jello he ate last night was still there.

Alla Blake wears thick black shoes her hair is thick and short she wears a watch she watches herself behind closed doors. She is alert.

Your sadness lives alongside you about the size of your purse when you open it you hear things deep down in there whispering so you keep it closed. There's a scratching sound in there too that frightens you. You buy a padlock and padlock the thing. It promises you the sun if only you'd remove the lock. No dice.

The goons are here in the yard again they want my hand in marriage. I love them but I lock myself in the house.

I'm with the fire department, lady. What's the trouble. "This door won't open." One of the goons let a lizard jump from his mouth. I said hold it fellas I wanna get my camera. They lady kept screaming so we locked her in the broom closet. When the kids came home in the Toyota they let her out. Then swept the floor and planted grass in the yard till the cops arrested them.

"There are thirteen million Jews four hundred and eight million Muslims and I don't know how many Confucianists and Buddhists and Hindus and Animists and Taoists and Shintoists and Atheists and . . . they all open and close doors all the time you see them stepping back and forth across thresholds." So?

The brilliant preacher confronts Sunday with church doors open.

The good life? Inlet may not be the best place for locating it. I tried dating Clara Bow strutting like Chaplin flying like Lindbergh negotiating like Dwight W. Morrow. I supported Margaret Sanger and read F. Scott Fitzgerald. I stood on Main Street and visited Hoover's Republic Club of Main at the museum. I fought for the farmer's rights and pushed for Smith. Alfred E., that is. I believed in socialized medicine and still could not feel the pulse of the so-called good life. I asked Jim if he knew anything about the good life and his answer was shattering: I feel only the throbbing of the secret current.

Unable to sleep Julie got up and sat by the candle, shivering in its light and opened her diary hoping she might feel compelled to scribble. Instead she began reading an early entry: *New York. Johnny & I asleep when phone rings & it's much distraught Hourari, African friend with whom I had brief frantic affair one weekend last yr. Says he's going to kill himself if he can't see me, right now. Jealous Johnny while I'm talking knocks phone out of my hand. Stupid anger. Picks up phone and tell Hourari I'll meet him downstairs in front of bldg. Johnny yells at me while I dress. So what. He's married and won't leave his pregnant wife, a white woman. Expects me to be just his standby. I must be free, not possessed. To love is not to be possessed. Met Hourari & we went up on roof of bldg. and in summer night breeze we fucked like minks. He felt better afterward. I felt better making him feel better. We then talked awhile & in the confusion of what he said I got impression he's being forced to return to Ghana. Didn't understand all the details. Poor unhappy Hourari. He left & I went down. Took shower & argued with Johnny till daybreak. He suspected what happened. Things are falling apart. Will I ever find the center of myself?*

They are lying together on the mattress and Julie rests her cheek against Al's chest. They are whispering. Remember how we met, she says. Yes, he says, it was a crazy party. Al, Julie says, I believe in being honest. It's the only thing I demand from a man because I demand it of myself and I know I love you Al so it is not a question of doubting that but lately I have begun to doubt all the things about us that I felt so sure about three weeks ago are suddenly so up in the air. I know, says Al. He feels Julie move, shift her weight. I told you about Jomo. Was he the Ghanaian. No, that was Julius. I lived with Jomo for a while when I was a student at the University of Ibadan. She let her tongue rest. There are only a few men I've truly loved deeply. As deeply as I love you and Jomo is one I often think of him and sometimes even after all this time since last seeing him, I feel very lonely for him he was so understanding. In some ways he's a lot like you one of the very few persons I've ever known who isn't so bound up in the cultural structure he was born to. And that when I was there in school was probably the most frustrating thing about African men they were so culturally bound but Jomo having lived in America for so many years broke away from a lot of his original social habits. She pauses. Jomo had a doormat that said welcome and Jomo was the musician right, says Al. Right, says Julie. He's a much older man than you maybe that's part of the reason we couldn't make it. Jomo was forty-five then and you're twenty-eight now I was only seventeen when I lived with him. That was four years ago and I can still see his face clearly in my mind and I miss him so much tonight oh so much. He used to leave notes for me tacked to his front door. I loved that they were little love

217

poems or sometimes lists of things to remember to do but poems just the same. And Jomo had sort of reached the point where he felt he didn't need anyone. Julie stops. The crickets outside sounded so close. I mean, she says, Jomo loved me I never will doubt that but he'd been through so much oh so much pain and suffering that he had built a wall around himself for protection from pain and it hurt me deeply when I finally realized that. Al strokes her hair. How long did you live with him. Only about two months but he opened many doors for me when I got out of school that summer I went across Africa to Kenya and to Nairobi where I met Julius he teaches there now but Julius always had a very fatherly attitude toward me and in many ways he was still very, very culturally bound do you know what I mean but Julius saved me from a terrible man once I'll never forget that night I thought I was goint to die. This African from Kampala I don't remember his name we'd all been at the beach that day and all day this African from Kampala had made it clear he wanted me and he knew I was with Julius but Julius was married at that time and though his wife wasn't on that occasion early on anywhere near the beach, he still had a very formal way of treating me in public, he was cool you know, respectful and everything and I found that in itself very annoying. Anyway this African from Kampala who was a friend of Julius asked me if he could drive me back to my hotel and it was after dark by then and since it seemed all right with Julius I thought it was okay too. I mean Julius had already whispered to me saying he was going to try to get away later that evening— his wife was there by that time and she had the children with her on the beach. But this Kampalan, instead of driving me to my place, forcefully took me out to his own house on the edge of town and when I argued with him he got brutal, when I resisted his attempt to make love to me he forced me out of the car. He twisted my arms and forced me into his house I fell trying to get away and I screamed but nobody heard me nobody came and at that point he just picked me up by my ankles and pulled me into his house just dragging me like that all the way into his bedroom and tore off my clothes and on the bed he threw me and kept trying to get on top of me but I fought him I fought him with everything I had in me but I got tired and was about to give in I was exhausted thinking it'd be easier to simply give in let him finish, then Julius came bursting into the room. So Julius had gone to my place and not finding me there assumed that this was what had happened apparently he knew this Kampalan was capable of such an act and Julius's arrival was the only thing that saved me. Though Julie's voice is high and thin as she narrates the story Al briefly puzzles over the quality of detachment that is obviously also in her attitude and voice. She goes on. Julius grabbed the wild African and they fought all over the place. When you were fighting this afternoon with that man the whole scene with the Kampalan came horribly back to me I had suppressed it for so long but it came back suddenly. Anyway Julius finally got me out of there and drove me home. That was the first night he ever spent the night with me and it ruined everything for him with his wife. She was very bitchy, an English lady and they had three children. And I think about six or seven months after that she left him returning to London took the kids with her. I'd gone back to Nigeria to finish school and when Julius wrote me about the separation I couldn't help but feel guilty you see when I got back to Jomo I told him all about Julius trying to be honest and it hurt him so deeply he cried so I couldn't say I mean stay there in his house watching him so moody and broken every day I was very stupid then very young and inexperienced. I mean it hurt me really hurt me to have caused such a beautiful person so much pain and to have wrecked Julius' marriage they were both beautiful men and I loved them both. Julie stops for a moment then goes on. I finished school without seeing Jomo again I don't blame him I don't ever again want to hurt anybody that much and yet I hate to lie I can't tell lies even by omission

220

yet if I'd lied to Jomo it would have saved him from the suffering I caused so sometimes I think it's impossible to have a good love relationship and at the same time be decent and honest in this world.

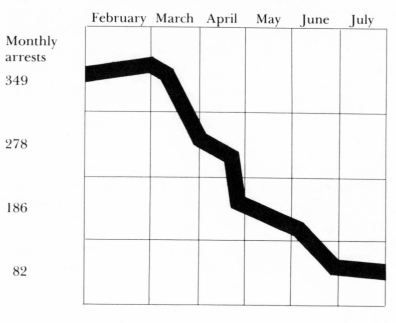

ACCEPTANCE OF THE NEW LAW?

Deborah is sitting up in bed again pale face. She's eating oatmeal from a blue plastic bowl. Her room is wide and shabby and dirty. The dog sleeping on the floor is snoring. Outside her window people are screaming with joy. They jump up and yell as loud as they can some are waving flags others ripping off their own clothes running through the streets.

All the shopping centers are empty. All the doors are locked. Rea and Dick are trying to find a drugstore. They are two runners suitable for scholastic study. So are Roslyn and Jim. So are Julius and his exwife.

The body has caved in on itself yet the person in it goes on seeing and understanding certain facts about the trees outside. This body belongs to me. I am it. I am beyond it. Yet I cannot be beyond it.

Right now a drunk Roslyn sits at a table with two drunk men. A fly is crawling into her open mouth. Jim has disappointed her again. She wants to cry.

They arrested a neighbor of Mrs. T. who was guilty of violating the threshold law ninety-nine times. But her husband was *more* guilty because that meant that he had not protected her from her violations. This is a news item. Is it six o'clock yet? The judge . . .

The crowd booed and heckled Jim threw rocks bottles at him and he said I have no sacraments no creeds. "I simply took my wife's hand when we got married. I carried her across the threshold she was not heavy, I swear to you she was light! . . ."

Julie reaches deep into the torn muscles where the heart is still beating. She eats it. Would dad disapprove? Why should he object?

Thousands of students at Inlet University are running naked across the grass. "My name," says one who stops long enough to talk to a reporter, "is Marlene. I always wanted to be a famous sexy bitchy movie star. Naughty boys like me are called delinquent. We do not necessarily represent the middle class. By the way, Rod Stewart is a friend of mine and I'm going to dedicate this next song to him and to my favorite movie star, Miss Marlene Dietrich!" *Yeeeeeeeeee!*

Hourari cuts into the nerve bed, eats the liver, the kidney then wipes his hands on the pelt then sleeps and dreams he's dead underground. Something is licking the tender parts of his body. He dreams of Julie. She's hard to separate from himself. He knows that it's not possible for her to be the same person he is yet he cannot pry her away from his sense of himself. There she is locked in him.

Smoking cigars and fingering the imaginary women Nicholas Zieff and the other men in the back office fart and laugh and belch and laugh while getting drunk. They've placed the Closed sign on the outer door so they feel pretty safe.

1. Barbara pulled off her wet raincoat and threw it on a chair then she lifted her yellow skirt.

2. Rose Marie got out of the boat and the boy followed her up to the old trapper's cabin. Inside it was completely dark.

3. Alla Blake got down on her knees to mumble into her own praying hands.

4. Patricia answered the phone and a man told her this is an obscene call then proceeded to tell her some things she had never heard before.

5. Barry Sands scratched his chin. Janice Page sipped the dry sherry from the narrow, bright glass.

6. Gordon called Patricia and they made a date for Sunday.

7. Jim and Roslyn met in a bar and went to her place.

8. Stella Della saw the Joe Rogers fight. She had an orgasm.

9. Deborah put on her bra and smiled in the mirror at herself. Her new lover was sitting on the side of his bed.

10. Leo looked up when the Moving Eye Clock struck one. The Negro eyeballs rolled from side to side. He chuckled and his wife walked in and caught him. What's so funny dinner is ready.

11. Janice Page has planned a secret meeting with Patrick Blake who is four years younger than she is. They meet at the Dewey Theatre, in the lobby. In the dark watching the soup line on the screen they hold hands. Walking her home he tells her about his lovely mom, Alla. She tells him about her troublesome relationship with a guy named Barry. In her apartment Patrick's erection is of special interest to Janice.

12. There is a relief parade outside my window. One woman in a hugh green coat carries a sign that says: apes at the zoo live on thirty-four cents a day the unemployed on twenty-five cents a day. The woman is marching with fifteen other citizens in a circle. When she turns I see her face for the first time. It's Deborah. I love Deborah.

13. Roslyn is having coffee with Jim. What's the difference between the CIO and the CIA. Jim gives her his unbelieving look.

As a bonus Allen Morris reveals amazing details about his past life, sure to please lovers of rounded characters. But is Al going to tell the truth?

Al is speaking now:

We were lying in the sun, stomachs down, on the raft anchored about thirty yards from the dyke. Julie's cheek was against her folded arm. Mine the same. The sun felt good on my back.

Do you realize, she said, I hardly know anything about you? I mean, like you've never mentioned your mother and father, what it was like when you were growing up, that sort of thing.

I guess it's because you never asked.

What was your father like?

A very ambitious man.

Your mother?

Sadie, my mother used to drag herself out of bed at six in the morning. This went on for ten years. She'd take the train to Long Island and walk to some rich white folks' home where she died a little bit each day she slaved for them on her knees. Scrubbing floors washing windows cleaning shit. And taking care of snotty nosed brats. Sadie always bragged to Joe and me how she ran the shit down to them about all the things she absolutely refused to do. From the start. But it didn't make any difference if she did light or heavy housework, spiritually it killed her either way. The weight is in the mind and the spirit.

My father, Joe, fought in World War Two and for many years was proud of it but around 1965 he stopped talking about it because the young Black people in our neighborhood started laughing at him. Like Sadie, he dropped out of school during the Depression. They never went to high school. Many doors were closed in their faces. My father had so many doors slammed in his face I think that's why his nose got so flat. When he got back from the war the people at the employment service told him he couldn't qualify for the kind of work he had done in the army. Get to that. He lived in New York in the Bronx then and they sent him back up town to see a man named Mr. Swadesh who owned a door manufacturing company. This man needed a janitor and Joe got the job cleaning toilets in a door company.

I grew up ashamed of both of them and was resentful and stayed away from home as much as possible. At first I had hope. I used to dream of becoming somebody and at one point I was an inventor. At another point a pilot. I even thought of becoming a superstar just to make enough money to make life easy for my parents. This was before I realized that the world is a shithole and most of the people in it are shitheads. When I was fifteen I was arrested for armed robbery and spent six months in a correctional institution in upstate New York. There, I learned how to handle myself in a dog-eat-dog environment. My job there was making doorknobs. Silver and gold painted doorknobs all day five days a week. When I got out my folks had moved, but we were still in Harlem.

I was eighteen and back on the streets and needed money so I hooked up with a dude who turned me on to a setup and I started pushing grass. H and snort was too heavy for me then. I layed into that for about a year and got to know everybody on the scene. A lot of country niggers hung out in the area. They weren't too bright. And it's still that way. People I had grown up with had scattered and new faces were always popping up. At first I tried to live at home but Sadie and Joe hassled me too much so I split.

With my own room in a nearby hotel I could have chicks stay overnight with me if I wanted to be in to that.

Then bam! I got drafted and went through basic training at San Antonio, Texas and got the chip knocked off my shoulder by the drill instructor who, with his buddies, one night cornered me in the dark between two barracks while I was pulling guard duty and while two of them held my arms he beat me in the face and stomach until I was a bloody slab of pain. You smartass New York nigger I should kill you. He kept saying that over and over as he beat me. I don't know how I survived two years in the army with racist white guys all around me. I got out having done only three months in the slam for lifting a camera off a white dude who shouldn't have left it lying around anyway.

Back in New York I attended City College for a few weeks before I realized that I was smarter than the teachers. I couldn't relate to what they were teaching so I quit. I walked out the door and never went back. Around this time I started seeing Gail. I hadn't seen her since elementary school. She was stupid naturally and got pregnant right away. I made her get an abortion and after that she hated me and everything went wrong. I don't know why we stayed together. It was a real sad life: we were just hurting each other and fighting and arguing all the time and we were hungry and poor, very poor.

Then she started playing tricks on me. She'd say, Allen, I'm going to the corner drugstore for a pack of smokes. And the bitch would be gone all night sometimes and then come dragging in half drunk in the morning. We broke up after one year then went back together. It was a mess. We kept breaking up and trying it again. She'd go live with her sister or mother then come back. I hated it all it was a stinking rotten life. I hated myself too. I wanted something better out of life and I knew the only way to get it would be to take it. I even thought once of robbing a bank. If I had had a good enough scheme I would have done it.

The Community I lived in in Harlem was too small and

hickified for me so I used to go down to the Village. I could sell shit down there and go back loaded and nobody knew my business.

Julie's smile was mysterious. "The only amazing thing about your confession, Al, is the fact that it is such a successful lie."

I hope a hundred years from now this book doesn't sound like *Vanity Fair*.

Barry Sandstone known as Barry Sands is in the hospital.

"Don't suppose I can eat anything. By the way did I get a call from somebody named Janice?"

"No to both."

"Is my rabbi here?"

"In fact, after surgery you won't *want* to eat. Maybe you'll never want to eat again."

"My rabbi. He promised to bring me a picture of a woman sitting in a doorway. I used to think the woman was my mother. Her first memory is like my own: warm and red. You're sure I can't have just a little ice cream."

"John Jackson Joe Smith and Jack Johnson Junior were arrested it says here in the *Daily News* they must be colored."

He closed his eyes. The first hypo was taking effect.

"I didn't know you were Jewish?"

"I still am. Janice used to suck me into her dreams and I'd always feel trapped."

The nurse laughed. "Even while she slept she could see you."

"How did you know? There is a light inside my head it makes my skull glow." He whimpered. Now speaking to himself: "She asks am I Jewish. I want a rabbi and she asks me am I Jewish. Does a chicken have an asshole does a bear shit in the woods am I Jewish."

"Just relax Mr. Sandstone you're going to surgery in twenty-five minutes."

Another nurse enters. "Give him his second hypo."

"He's pretty much under the anesthetic now."

"Yes, but he's still strong."

"I feel fine. I could rope a calf. I could ride a horse named Bill."

The "butcher shop" was freezing and he was going fast then it was all dark. He was out of it.

When he came back the pain was first to greet him. He was halfway back and somewhere in an afternoon landscape drenched with sunlight that had turned everything red. Trees, the nuns, the road, the meadow, everything was yellow red. A Brancusi stone was half hidden beneath an oak. Wind blew in from the planes. A galloping horse entered the clearing. Across its back hung the bleeding body of Barry dressed as an Ottawa.

"Have I had the operation?"

"He's beginning to come to."

"Don't try to talk Mr. Sandstone."

"Where am I?"

"Don't talk. You're in recovery. Al and Julie are not in love did you know that."

The surgeon turned to the nurse who made that comment. "What's the matter with you are you out of your mind keep your eye on this patient."

"Yes, Doctor."

"Give him a hypo."

She gives it to him and how. "Take this and this. Remember when I was a kid I searched for my own orgasm it was always hiding in the back of a locked closet or down in the basement behind the furnace where Bigger Thomas burned the body."

"My rabbi?"

"Don't talk." She placed a finger over her closed lips. "Do you want to be a dog warden or a farmer don't answer just listen."

He was too weak to answer so he tried to smile.

She loved having a captive audience of one. She went on. "When the doorbell rang I hid the shotgun. It was not the person I expected. It was Dr. Feinstein. He wanted me to go out with him said his wife was mean."

"Janice. Who is Al who is Julie."

"You're trying to talk again. Cool it Mr. Sandstone cool it or I'll have to knock you out completely. Doctor's orders."

"I'm in pain."

"I'll put you in a bubble of snot hanging from the nose of the president and you'll never be the same."

"Recovery?"

"Okay you're asking for it."

The needle injection sends him away. He's resting with his back against a tree. The American flag flies above his head. Next to him is a charming, delightful, lovely girl in a mini dress. She stands up and walks away so gracefully he forgives her for leaving. She's so light on her high heels, with her head thrown back, she walks swiftly along with a slight bounce, with an even slighter wiggle. He calls her Julie but she doesn't answer. I ask her where is she from she says a place called Janice. Where's that. In Germany. But she doesn't have a German accent. How come.

"Hi Doc."

"You can go home tomorrow."

"Home?"

First a woman is sitting in the dim doorway of a thatched roof house. Jim is painting her as part of the background for The Great Tree. On closer inspection I realize the woman is Julie's mother and she is in a trance. With the eyes in her head she sees the wall that separates her life from her other life. Her first memory is red and cold, wet and warm.

Early in the morning when nobody's watching giant Hollywood bugs crawl on the horizon eating the rust from the bridges and drinking pissy sewer water. This hurts the economy.

"Skylights and chimneypots have captured me completely."

"Janice used to suck me into her dreams and I'd always feel trapped." Even while she slept she could see me.

O Photographers are taking pictures of the demonstration. O dear!

"I'm holding a group of ideas hostage in exchange for a set of new assumptions." What? "We were working in a traveling circus we each had an act we had to do." *What?*

The door is about to close there is no place like the moving platform at fourteenth street the voice keeps saying step back from the moving platform year after . . . When in New York Julie listens to it.

We are running trying to catch the shuttle the clang beating inside our bodies. Bats beat their wings in Inlet bird cages.

Police report: these persons were arrested today: John Jackson John Scott John Johnson Jack Johnson Joe Louis Joe Smith Joe Smith Junior John Smith and Jack Johnson Junior.

I stop for a beer Roslyn and Jim are doing the tango they are naked and sweating. A picture of Van is on the bottle his eyes are tortured.

Entering this place, there is a light inside my head it makes my eyes glow.

Farmer working alone on a cloudy day. I sit beneath a tree. I have no shoes. In town Elmer Blake is teaching a gorilla to paint pictures.

Dark figure against a hazy purple skyline, a massive church, tiny in the distance. Black purple earth.

"I watch you watching them and watch them watching you."

Thousands wander around bumping into each other they tremble. All doors everywhere are locked. There is no place to hide.

The sermon today is the fate of a young woman who took it upon herself to go down from a road to say hay hello to a bunch of wild horses.

The minister stands at the door to greet the church-comers.

In the seaside house Deborah fully dressed sketches Roslyn, a naked woman. Outside in the yard there is a consistently low scraping sound and at least at first it's disruptive. Jim and the children are away.

There is a yellow light that clouds the whole area. People are away on vacation some are in Italy asking foolish questions.

Rose Marie and Oscar are in the trapper's cabin whispering to each other in the darkness. Which social and economic crises do you like best he says. She says I like the fights between the American Federation of Labor and the Congress of Industrial Organizations. Oh golly says Oscar a woman after my own heart! At this point the natural thing happens: they hug each other.

A team of police are beating demonstrators. Six or seven men are sprawled on the sidewalk bleeding. Barry Sands is one of them. He believes in equality of the sexes and the races it's a costly outlook.

The minister stands at the door as the congregation leaves.

Deborah in the little house talking to Al: Jim's taken a room in a nearby motel it's accessible to the building in which he works despite his indecision I really think he'll go to her in the end just a feeling and I've been trying to imagine what life will be like without him I'm no longer young I mean I'm older now for a woman I'm old and I seriously don't think my chances of finding another man the kind I want who'll sweep me off my feet and carry me across the threshold the kind I want to spend the rest of my life with are any too good see most men you know I'd be interested in want women younger than me see I'm trying to be realistic I mean if I were to become involved with a younger man say someone your age I'd never know whether or not he truly cared about me as a person or was simply with me for material reasons that is assuming he'd have less in those terms than I have oh Al it's very difficult.

She jerked her head up looking sideways at him resting on her elbows. Her eyes were already swollen from crying and she started crying again.

She was stretched out on the mattress and he sat along-side her looking out through the screen.

Anyway, she said, I still have Oscar and I still have to be a mother to him that gives me something to live for the girls don't really need me anymore so I have to see Oscar through to the point when he'll be going away to college—if he goes one of the things I appreciate about Oscar is he knows how to occupy himself even how to cook for himself he's a good solid boy and I'm not worried about him it's myself I'm worried about really what'll happen to *me* see I don't want to be like those middle-aged women I hear about whose husbands leave or die they suddenly find themselves chasing young men and going crazy the so-called gay divorcee god knows I don't want to be like that so I have to think realistically about what's happening of course I'd rather spend the rest of my life with Jim but he doesn't want me well . . .

Deborah's one syllable laugh was joyless.

Besides, she said, Roslyn *is* very attractive any man would enjoy lifting her across a threshold or two and though she's no spring chicken she's younger than me and well you know how some Black men are about white women and how some white women are about Black men and I'm afraid Jim is like that and Roslyn is like that then on the other hand they might be attracted to each other on a purely human level who knows why any two people are attracted to each other any way anyway Jim maintains that her color has nothing to do with it he says he loves her for the person she is and wants a life with her which leaves me where all by my lonesome.

Deborah closes her eyes and when she opens them Al is not there.

Deborah went to the big house around ten and Al read a detective novel until midnight. Take me to your leader. That was its title. In her bed in the bighouse Deborah was also reading. Go tell it in the basement. Then bored she watched the 60's on TV. An incident in the film reminded her of an incident at age seven: she wiped a kiss off her school desk. It had been planted there by the boy who sat next to her. He was a pain in the ass.

Julie came home from work at twelve thirty. She said, That place is getting to be a pain in the ass.

I must make a confession: I'm in love with Deborah. I tried to keep it to myself but the feeling in me is a storm. Listen. I'm with Deborah now, finally. I'm on the sidewalk watching her large pink breasts dangling from the window of a fleabag hotel. Deborah in a fleabag hotel? I'm distressed by this. (I once stayed in a fleabag hotel and in the middle of the night watched a fancy film maker and his crew making a movie about a heartbroken wealthy guy who has retreated to a fleabag hotel to feel sorry for himself.) But now Deborah has no head no legs. Just breasts with large pink nipples. I'm stuck here watching them.

"... I lifted my eyes to the tiers of volumes and false doors covered with imitation book-backs which surrounded that focus of learning . . ."

—Ezra Pound,
Guide to Kulchur

"'You think I could become a tree?'
'That all depends.'"

—Renate Rasp,
A Family Failure

". . . He took one look then went out the back window just ahead of the police. . . ."

—William Carlos Williams,
Paterson

Well,
dear reader,
how do
you feel
about it?

They hadn't been asleep two hours when Deborah
came in and woke them to say goodbye. She was leaving the
summer house till next weekend heading for the regular
house and her job as secretary in the mayor's office.

Deborah kissed Julie then looked over at Al whose
back was turned. How about a kiss kiddo.

Sure, Deborah. But he didn't move.

Suddenly Julie screamed then yelled, What's the
matter with you, Al, mom asked you for a kiss and you lay
there ignoring her what in the fuck is wrong with you
anyway!

Al was sure now that this was the end. This is the end.
This is the way it ends. This was the first time she'd shouted
at him. This was surely the end. He peeped out to see her
face. The same contempt in her voice was on her face.

And Deborah sat there on her knees looking sympathetic.
She too knew the end was in sight. What could she say.
What could she say. What could anybody do or say. The
end is the end.

Deborah kissed Al then left. They heard her drive
away and as they listened Julie said to Al, It's ending isn't it.

A dagger is thrown through Jim's hand. His hand falls onto a blue shield. The shield is attached to the back of a huge white rat. The rat attacks a naked man nailed to a cross. The man smiles says forgive them for they know nothing—they were only playing. Who is they. A large detached breast shakes its nipple at a mob of men and women caught in the act of breeding. They run away in despair with many tiny bugs and ants scurrying at their feet. Small deformed animals with dog whiskers scatter beneath bushes and ruins. There is suddenly a threshold of grass to the forest.

Every time somebody kills somebody the crowd cheers you can tell it's all in fun the way the arrows keep going through various people who came here to see what would happen.

You are a potter in jeans and t-shirt and thick, worn work boots you wear a wool cap. You sit on a tiny firm chair, legs crossed, holding a clay pot. You squint as you hold it close making it smoother. It's propped on your huge belly. Now you're drawing with a nail tiny squares all over it they each are passages to your own mystery which is as hollow as the pot.

Three hundred and twenty-seven 1974 Buicks are lined up along the curb bumper to bumper. Nobody's in them. The sky overhead is hazy. Trees along the sidewalk are sunk in fog. Coming this way Jim Ingram is carrying a shoe box. In it is this exact scene all over again, only this time in his box, it takes place in the hallway near the door of his home. He lives at the end of this street. His wife right now is asleep under the bed. Her belly is warm her breasts are warm the space between her breasts is warm. He closes his eyes as he walks, seeing his wife's thighs, the space between them. It is warm there too. He opens himself and finds a passageway. It is warm there, too. He can't wait to get home to make sure everything is still changing, appearing the same. The cars? He starts counting the cars. The doors on the cars. The windows. Before he knows for sure, he is entering his own home. A car, with four doors, is parked in the living room. In the back seat his wife is making love to a picture of Tom Mix.

The sunlight falls along the rickety old fence made of crooked tree limbs. It hits the back of Roslyn's head. She's sitting on an orange crate knitting a dark blue shawl.

Hello over there. The little girl near Roslyn does not answer. A man appears and pushes his way through the weeds. Where is the line? At what point will Roslyn or the girl lift her head and focus her eyes in desperate anger.

Fancy horses prance in a field nearby. Fancy horses trot in a field near the clear eye of each.

A bull behind them chewing grass. People behind the bull crowded at the gate buying tickets for the final competition.

Two pretty little girls named Julie and Barbara pose for a snapshot in the last light.

Cora Oni and Helen eat mushrooms baked with ruby leaves and Chinese pac-choy mustard spinach baked with peas called wandoes. Barbara and Windy and Henry eat chicken. Barry eats ice cream and pumpkin pie. Nobody's eating the toejam radishes shelled sunflower seeds.

The sailors are still strutting around hoping to find stray girls. Old women turn up their noses. Their faces are red with cosmetics they wear large green hats some are here visiting from another part of the world many have relatives here businessmen in business suits walk fast along the sidewalks fearful of something nobody's defined yet firemen pull out their firehoses streetcleaners are pushing early morning carts along.

Now that I know that the good life does not exist I am searching for the main artery that wiggles its way through the trauma called Inlet. At least I might have the satisfaction of understanding what is going on around me. It *can* happen here. Walking along Main Street I see the body fascists doing their running. The Nazi techniques of my neighbors no longer frighten me. Their target practice is like a puppy without a trumpet. Migratory workers on the outskirts of town are sleeping in their own pee pee and doo doo. Where is the New Deal. Jim answers me: we have a committee studying the situation do you wish to be in on the decision making process.

When Julie came in Al was in bed but not asleep. When she got in bed he reached for her but she pushed his hand away. Do you remember the carpenter I told you about who comes in to get drunk every night at the bar. He told her he remembered. Well, Julie said, tonight he asked me to join him for a drink and tonight was the first time he came in with friends. Usually he comes in alone and gets smashed and goes home I guess he goes home. He always seemed sort of out of place among the summer stock theatre crowd that hangs around the Pussy. Anyway he leaves very large tips something like twenty-five percent. Tonight there were these three guys with him. Not his type at all. Sort of brash arrogant young men and I told you he's about my father's age he even looks like my father a little except he's white. I guessed those younger guys worked with him maybe they work *for* him. Right now he told me they are building thresholds by the thousands by the thousands all kinds even thresholds of gold and diamonds it's a booming business. Anyway he asked me this carpenter asked me to join him for a drink and I told him I'd be happy to when things weren't so busy so later I got the chance and I sat with them sat next to him and while I was sitting there he was telling me the sorry sad story of his life and how bitchy his wife is and all the troubles he's having with her then he stopped talking and his arrogant friends starting making passes at me they really turned me off. Anyway the carpenter was just looking at me and then he suddenly said, You know I'm making love to you Julie making love to you right now and wow, I understand why he had to say that and what he meant I mean I already knew it from the look in his eyes I don't know if you can understand this Al or if you can accept it but I felt his hand under the table and I knew why he had to touch me at that moment. I don't know maybe I shouldn't tell you this but he stuck his finger in and I let him and I wasn't offended but I would have been offended had he been another type but he's really very gentle and very sad and it was no big thing to let him do it it was just something he had to do at that moment and I understood it and accepted it and he smiled and it made him happier and it didn't cost me anything to give him that little bit of happiness. Do you can you understand what I'm trying to say?

Al did not answer.

I'm trying to get to know Deborah better. Outside her house a storm is coming down into the ocean. Maybe Deborah is my woman the one I started out with. Did she grow up on Puss in Boots and Count Screwloose and Mutt and Jeff. I once talked with her about Hans and Fritz the Katzenjammer kids of 1918. She's old enough to remember. Remember? She brushed her hair back from her face. Her mouth opened but no words. Her mouth is so beautiful. Now. White teeth. Strong jaw. Pretty knees showing where her robe falls away. We're sipping coffee and touching toes beneath the table. She's my favorite character in this whole book. It's Fall.

Deborah called and said she needed Julie to be with her. Julie slid into her jeans and Al combed his hair with his pick.

They got started around noon and it was a clear day. They took the back roads. Julie dropped Al off in Harlem. Tears were streaming down her pink cheeks. He stroked her hair and kissed her and promised to call her. He was pretending that the end was not truly here.

She drove away fast.

A wind storm is raging outside. Deborah has become my lover. I'm not so blue any more. Deborah is idealistic and mature and motherly. She holds my face when she kisses me. She has a pleasant disposition.

We go to bed and #%¢&@+ for hours!

I'll never try to sell Deborah a threshold!

The people coming this way have scars on their necks. It is whispered they came here from some place farther east. Never talk to anybody except themselves. If you look directly into their eyes there is a blinding light that shines from their pupils.

The Scottish Presbyterian Church at Broad and Church mysteriously disappeared last night nobody speaks of it. South Church which used to face Main over night turned around on its own and now faces Hale this happened just today nobody has said a word about it. Shhh.

Deborah returned to the seaside house carrying seven empty cans. There was no more water. Barbara and Julie started crying.

I'm with Jim again in his bedroom in a rooming house in Inlet. I'm near the door he's near the window. We've been here since I discovered I have visions too. I wait for him to speak he's waiting for me to introduce myself. I figure I have to have a good story. So I tell him I sell thresholds for joyrides and sumptuous thresholds. I have charts showing our warehouse clearance sale on thresholds. A gem of a sale spectacular threshold values but I wait for the right moment to whip out my real offer. Jim goes on preoccupied with his room watching the light change I'm careful not to break the spell ruin the sale at the right moment I can sell him a hundred thresholds pear-shaped opal-studded thresholds thresholds trimmed in emeralds Baroque pearl-studded thresholds ruby- and jade-studded thresholds oval- aquamarine-studded thresholds yellow sapphire thresholds thresholds the color of dracaena or California cactus thresholds cyprus papyrus thresholds! Finally I smile. He does not return my smile. He's saying something in French I ask him to repeat he repeats in Dutch I still don't understand something about old women down at the church gate making the sign of the cross every time they see Jomo drink from his bottle in the churchyard. See here I say finally do you suppose you might be interested in a new gateway complete with a walkway leading from this room down to where Jomo is sprawled in arrogant despair.

They fed that possessed woman ice cream and cake her body was swollen fifty or sixty people sucked at her mouth and vagina and anus and nose and eyes. Things were nasty out there in that vacant lot where she lay on a rusty cot. After twelve hours she gave them a loud fart and they all went home. She died from cancer anyway and was reborn ten years later as a nurse in Bloomfield New Jersey working the night shift.

Now Oscar and Patrick and the other boys line up at the soda fountain trying to remember what it was they wanted to do. Dreamy look in the eye. Blue leather jacket. Thin lips quivering. A thug. The music is straight out of cheese-burger heaven the boys dream of a rose in Spanish Harlem of skyscrapers greenlit backrooms of pool players sharp as tacks Tina Turner making that sucking sound of snatch of being a lonesome fugitive of strawberry hills and fields forever of Sally as she goes around the roses of rebels of the guitar man of Brenda Lee of Claudette of shooting a man in Reno of honky tonk angels of stealing a car of getting laid in the back seat of a car of tuning into a werewolf of getting drunk of . . .

"Hard work and clean living my folks came here my grand-parents the Quakers the Indians the Puritans nobody knows the troubles you get your reward in . . . violence well you see in them days news didn't get about so fast so we've been here since the cow jumped over the moon."

Elmer Blake (in his dream) takes care of the mules and has not looked into the face of another person in over thirty years. He likes it this way.

Johnny Hawkins, who was never really in the story, is angry and he is taking it out on Julie: "I want a piece of the action, a piece of the pie, a piece of ass, a piece at a time, a piece of land, a piece, and peace of mind!" Julie does not know how to respond. She thought he had all these things already. Besides if the researcher is watching her she does not want to give the wrong answer.

1. Al knocks on a door. Printed on it are these words: *Staff Only.* The building that contains the door is a stage prop. There is no staff of life there.

2. Julie opens a door that says: *Authorized Personnel Only.* She is alone. It's an employment office and there are no authorized persons in the room she enters.

3. Jim approaches his own office door. *Warning! Hazardous Area.* Roslyn is there in the office typing a letter to the CIA.

4. Barbara scratches her brow while standing before the swing-door of a drugstore. She reads its message: *We Speak English Spanish French.* She speaks only English, though she can read Spanish and French.

5. Roslyn cleans her sunglasses while standing before a door that says *Stay Clear of Doors.* She's on the New York subway going to Macy's.

6. Barry is rushed to the hospital. Something is wrong with him. He is in pain. Pain is a signal. They carry him in a wheelchair through the Emergency Entrance. Letters on the door: *Emergency Door.*

7. Janice struts up to a trap door. She has a bucket of white paint in her left hand. With her right, she paints on the door: *Beware of Dog.* When she finishes she barks and laughs.

8. Al sees a side door. *Keep Out.* He goes in. It's the

Ingram home. He thinks he must be dreaming.

9. Julie is shopping in the Inlet Mall. She approaches a stairway to a lower level. Painted on the door: *Watch Your Step*. She looks at the step and decides that it is not hers. Not to keep.

10. Barbara sees a large blue door. *Knock Before Entering*. She enters without knocking. It's the office of her father's boss: he runs the country's intelligence agency. Barbara wants to know what's up.

11. Jim instructs his secretary to post a notice on the office door: *No Salesmen*. Salesmen from everywhere suddenly arrive.

12. Roslyn dreams that her apartment door is the beginning of a dangerous area. Posted on the outside: *No Trespassing*.

13. One door: *In*. The other: *Out*. Jim doesn't know which way to go. He stands half way between them, puzzled.

14. Deborah is interested in something new. She speaks: "Secret panel doors have saved many lives."

15. At age fifteen Julie told her mother: "Shut your trap."

16. Jim wants to buy Roslyn a present. He goes shopping in downtown Inlet. He sees several shops for women. They have door signs: *We Are Open*.

17. Roslyn wants to do the same for Jim. She approaches a man's shop. Its door says: *Sorry We Are Closed*. It leaves her frustrated so she buys an ice cream cone. One with ice cream on it.

18. Al is working as a delivery boy. He goes through an

alley to a side door. *Ring Bell for Service.*

19. Deborah wants to buy herself a new coat. She goes to the best ladies' shop in town. The door says: *Come In and Browse Around.*

20. Julie takes Poot with her into town. She feels hungry and decides to stop at Nick's for a snack. On the door, these words: *No Pets.*

NC
NC
GENCY
ERGENCY
EMERGENCY
EMERGENCY LA
NG EMERGENCY LAN
NDING EMERGENCY LAN
ANDING EMERGENCY LA
LANDING EMERGENCY LA
Y LANDING EMERGENCY LA
Y LANDING EMERGENCY LA
NCY LANDING EMERGENCY LA
ENCY LANDING EMERGENCY L
GENCY LANDING EMERGENCY L
RGENCY LANDING EMERGENCY
RGENCY LANDING EMERGENC
RGENCY LANDING EMERGEN
RGENCY LANDING EMERGE
RGENCY LANDING EMERG
ERGENCY LANDING EMERG
ERGENCY LANDING EMER
MERGENCY LANDING EME
EMERGENCY LANDING EM
EMERGENCY LANDING E
RGENCY LANDING
ENCY LANDIN
ENCY LANDIN
EMERGE
ERGE
RG
E
E
E
EE
E EEE
E EEE
E
E
E

ERG
EMERGE
LANDING EMERGE
MERGENCY LANDING EMERGE
G EMERGENCY LANDING EMERGE
DING EMERGENCY LANDING
LANDING EMERGENCY LAN
NCY LANDING EMERGENCY LAND
GENCY LANDING EMERGENCY LA
RGENCY LANDING EMERGENCY L
RGENCY LANDING EMERGENCY
MERGENCY LANDING EMERGENC
EMERGENCY LANDING EMERGE
MERGENCY LANDING EMERG
ERGENCY LANDING
EMERGE
MERGE
ERG
RG
G
E
E
E
E
E
E

EMERGENCY
EMERGENCY L
MERGENCY LAN
RGENCY LAND
GENCY LANDIN
GENCY LANDING EMERGENCY
ENCY LANDING EMERGENCE
ENCY LANDING EMERGENCE
NCY LANDING EMERGEN
LANDING EMERGE
ING EMERGE
MERGE
ERG
RG
G
E
E
E
E
E

EMER
G EMERGENCY
EMERGENCY L
MERGENCY LAN
RGENCY LAND
GENCY LANDIN
GENCY LANDING
ENCY LANDING
ENCY LANDING
NCY LANDING

254

1. In a small house in the countryside the author was dying at an early age then he recovered and nobody knew why or how.

2. During his illness he slept with a huge Dracaena Messangeana plant near his bed. He was its namesake.

3. His wife Deborah stayed in the kitchen she found him so repulsive. They felt they had known each other too long.

4. Beyond the window of the bedroom where he spent all his time there was a row of pecan trees and beyond it an apple orchard with honeysuckle at the far side. Bees and flies and birds and chickens and dogs made their sounds all day and at night frogs and crickets and other night callers were heard. Nobody brought him a bowl of figs from the fig tree on the other side of the house.

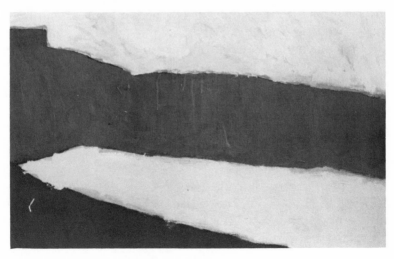

5. Deborah made cakes in the kitchen and slept there in a corner and read the newspapers to find out about new deaths and new laws. The Threshold Law did not interest her. When the articles about it started appearing in the newspapers she merely skimmed them then went on to the deaths which she read very carefully.

6. Then the day finally came. He was found on the floor looking for his shoes. His wife found him. She was on her way to get the newspaper which had just been thrown against the front door when she saw him—she called him Drama—on the floor with his nose under the bed.

7. What's the trouble she said.

8. I want to go out across that threshold into the sunlight. Where are my kicks? Then he spotted them.

9. No sir said his wife you can't wear your Sunday shoes. If you go you go barefoot.

10. So he made his way across the threshold not only barefoot but half naked. A few hundred interested characters in this very novel stood around in his neighborhood waiting for this earth-shaking event. Drama was taking command! he was coming out.

11. Directly in front of the house there was open warfare. One army was on the far side of the highway and the other on the near. The highway itself was the battleline. A stray round of bullets ate a circle in the porch wall near his head. He stopped moving.

12. These are the hostile armed forces he said aloud to himself. Yet he would not turn back. He'd come this far and sunlight was only a few feet away. Only a coward would retreat. He did not know the issues they fought over.

13. The soldiers did not know the issues either.

14. A lot of dead soldiers were lying in the street. As he crawled alongside them he read their name tags. None of them were familiar. Names like: Allen Rea Elmer Blake Steve Nicholas Zieff Julie Johnny Hawkins Tony Deborah Ron Hal Charles Vic Dick Patricia Barry Phillip Barbara Albert Jim Oscar Nikki Patrick Anki Van David Frank Eddie Janice Richard Clarence Pete Joe Paul John Cindy Jerry Kute.

15. Flat on his belly he crawled to the side along the wall headed for the driveway alongside the house. Deborah watched him from the doorway. She held her breath. What a brave fella. She didn't know he had it in him. Knock on any door.

16. He reached the fence and the pecan trees without being shot but he wasn't yet in sunlight. Only a few more inches to go. His knees were aching and his head felt heavy and his eyes burned. He could hardly breathe.

17. To reach the first inch of sunlight he'd have to crawl through a narrow hole in a fence. It seemed easy till he got half way through. Trying to bend back a tough piece of wire he cut his hand. His left leg received a deep cut from the other side. His knees were also beginning to bleed.

18. The warring troops were now exchanging fire with even more zest.

19. Drama looked back at them and realized that the dead ones had gotten up and rejoined the fight. Perhaps they were all using blanks. Just playing a game of fiction.

20. Through the gunfire he heard his wife calling him.

21. To hell with her.

22. He continued.

23. The minute he reached the warm light of the sun he began to burn. First the right arm then his face and left arm. Also the part of his chest not covered by the nightgown. Little flames began to leap from his face and arms. But he did not stop.

1972-1979

FICTION COLLECTIVE
Books in Print:

Clarence Major is the prize-winning author of four novels, five collections of poems, a critical study of Black American literature, a dictionary of Afro-American slang, and editor of an anthology. His works have been translated into German, Italian, French, Spanish and other languages and he has been the recipient of grants from the National Council on the Arts, the State Department, the New York Cultural Foundation and the Holland Festival in Rotterdam. Major's poetry won the 1976 Pushcart Prize and his shorter works appear in over a hundred anthologies and periodicals. Major teaches literature and creative writing and gives lectures and readings at universities and colleges around the country.